CW01497987

ANARCHY!

OZIAS PLUME SAVES THE WORLD

A novel by Daisy Waugh

Fisher King Publishing

ANARCHY!

A CIP catalogue record for thise book is available from the British Library.

Published by
Fisher King Publishing
fisherkingpublishing.co.uk

Cover design and illustrations by Panda La Terriere

Printed and bound by CPI Group (UK) Ltd. Croydon, CR0 4YY

MIX
Paper | Supporting responsible forestry
FSC® C013604

In memory of my brother Alexander,
always and forever ahead of the joke.

With enormous love.

NEW 'LAUGHING SICKNESS' MYSTIFIES SCIENTISTS

DAILY TELEGRAPH

BRITISH AUTHORITIES ON HIGH ALERT AS MYSTERY 'LAUGHING BUG' CAUSES CIVIC DISRUPTION

The New York Times

MISERABLE BRITS CAN'T STOP LAUGHING

NEW YORK POST

SERIOUSLY, IT'S NO JOKE!

Daily Mail

HEY NUMBNUTS, GET A GRIP!

THE SUN

BBC MORNING NEWS, LIVE INTERVIEW WITH THE PRIME MINISTER OF BRITAIN

PM: Like many people, I myself enjoy a little chuckle every now and then. We all do, don't we? We enjoy a little giggle sometimes. But we enjoy *appropriate* little chuckles and giggles at *appropriate* times.

BBC: Appropriate chuckles at appropriate times! I don't think anyone would argue with that!

PM: The key word is 'appropriate'. We can't, at this point, simply permit *anyone* to chuckle about *anything*. That isn't an option.

BBC: So the message is: Not all laughter is funny.

PM: *Not all laughter is funny.* That's right. And we really need to work *together* to get that message home.

BBC: *Not all laughter is funny.*

PM: This is what the Public Inquiry will be focusing on. While also firmly putting to bed some of the really quite ludicrous misinformation that's been circulating.

BBC: Hmm. Yes. I think a lot of our listeners will be very much behind you on this, Prime Minister!

PM: The message is: Appropriate laughter, *yes.* Inappropriate, cruel or harmful laughter, *no.*

BBC: And what about *fines*, Prime Minister? For those who don't or won't comply? Will there be *fines*? ...

INAPPROPRIATE OR HARMFUL LAUGHTER WILL <u>NOT</u> BE TOLERATED

NOT ALL LAUGHTER IS FUNNY

If you witness a laughter incident text 61016. In case of emergency call 999.

#FightThisTogether

MAYOR OF LONDON

£6,400 MAXIMUM FINE

1

THE PUBLIC INQUIRY, DAY ONE

Ozias Plume sits gazing at his phone, in the middle
of a room arranged to suit the set up: something
between a lawcourt, an airport lounge and an
upmarket boardroom. Very boring. Also in the
room, representing the world's media, sits an
unusually large bank of reporters. This is because
Ozias Plume is unlike the room he sits in. He is a
very interesting man, for many reasons.

Age: 43
Nationality: unknown
Skin: very shiny.
Family background: itinerant, obscure,
impecunious.
Body: 7/10. Good height. Lean and sporty.
Handsomeness: 6/10. Hair had been thinning,
seems lately to be springing back to life.
Financials: unknown.
Marital status: unclear.
Interestingness: to be revealed. His name has
been the most searched on Google for three years
in a row. Not that this is necessarily an indicator.

In front of Ozias, on a beige carpeted dais, behind a
long table, inside an integrated but fully enclosed
glass-fronted cube, sit the panellists: two adult

ladies and an adult gent, dressed mostly in blues and greys. They each have a microphone in front of them, a clean tumbler wrapped in cellophane, and four unopened mini bottles of water.

Directly behind Ozias are the Everyday Benches – about eight of them altogether. Space for approx. 60 everyday people. The benches are packed.

And behind the everydays, encased in a raised and integrated glass cube similar to, but less luxurious than, the panellists' cube at the opposite end of the room, sit the reporters, the spads, the spin doctors and the lobbyists – aka (without irony) the Vested Parties. It's a bit of a sardine situation in the VP Box this morning. But occupiers' concerns have been soothed with the provision of cellophane-wrapped tumblers etc, as per the other box. Also, the media/VP Box, like the Panellists' Box, has its own independent air conditioning system. All is well. No one is complaining, or not yet.

For the past several minutes Ozias, who shares the air with the Everyday Benches, has been exchanging affectionate messages with Debs Malone from Reading, 43yrs. She sits a few rows behind him. Something salacious just popped into Deb's mind. She's sent Ozias a message, updating him. She watches as he receives it. Notices his shoulders moving.

He and Debs are both trying not to giggle.

They may well not be the only ones. Bubbling beneath the sombre hum, in this incredibly boring room, there is a silent note, a bit like an irritating but playful wasp (a silent one) and it's hard to know, of the 150-plus humans present, which among them are already in on the so-called joke. In the early stages, in a place like this, people tend to try very hard to keep it hidden.

But let's start with the panel. The grown ups in the room. We can safely say they are not in on the joke and haven't been in on any joke for some time.

Jeremy, Davina and Sensible Su nestle behind their innocuous names. Su's father was a Jamaican-born ne'er do well who died in 1996, in prison. Davina is a late-to-life lesbian from Hillingdon who, many years ago, played ping pong for her country (Team-GB). And Jeremy was sent to boarding school when he was eight. But in other respects, they are similar. Though they vote for different parties and have drifted from different gods, their variously sized and shaded buttocks are steeped in very much the same butter. They work reasonably hard – or they did, once. They earn exceptionally well and one way or another have accrued a lot of wealth. They go to restaurants. They have family lives, and at home, awaiting their return, they each have a housekeeper, and a dog.

Other things they have in common: monikers that highlight their distinguished careers. Jeremy's full name is Lord Stevens of Dirkmass and Stirton. He was ennobled for services to social health, ostensibly. Or possibly Law. On the other hand, he may be a recently retired

diplomat. Davina Dewan is a dame, ennobled for services not to ping pong but the civil service. And Su Lee, the youngest of the three, already has an MBE because of her amazing work in charity, and is due to get her damehood imminently, or so she has been assured. This, though, will have less to do with her amazing charity work and more to do with her political affiliations/ donations – etc.

Other things they have in common—

Put it this way— to any visiting Martian (good on identifying human vibes but fuzzy when differentiating our physical details), these three Panel Members would appear more or less identical. Which fact – and it is a fact - Jeremy, Davina and Sensible Su, picked for their diversity, would have refuted strongly. They might even have sniggered in the Martian's 'face', since they are generally exempt from everyday fines. "Truth hurts", the Martian might have replied.

But Jeremy, Davina and Sensible Su wouldn't have listened. They are long past the stage where they entertain fresh ideas from anyone, least of all from a Martian.

2

In any case, our panellists are (of course) different in many subtle ways. For example: two of them are women, and one is a man. They also differ in age. At 72, Jeremy – or Lord Stevens of Dirkmass and Stirton – is the oldest by several years. Also the slimmest. He can still fit into his first-wedding trousers: a feat, had either been wearing trousers on those fateful days, that the Dame/s-In-Waiting could only imagine. Lord Stevens of Dirkmass and Stirton puts his trim figure down to the golf, which he plays whenever his schedule allows. But it's probably not as simple as that. He also has a much younger, second wife, who bosses him around and won't let him eat gluten.

Dame Davina is 61 years old and chubby (to put it mildly). She is on her first wife but her second spouse. Both have proved disappointing. Like the Dame-in-Waiting (Sensible Su), she is mother to two children now in their late twenties. Unlike the Dame-in-Waiting, whose children are apparently doing splendidly, neither of Dame Davina's children are in solid relationships, nor in jobs that Dame Davina considers valid.

The Dame-in-Waiting, (sensible) Su MBE, who's done a lot for charity, is married to a man who made a fortune in eco-housing during the nineties and noughties, and who, after 35 years of marriage, does a good job of mostly avoiding her. Dame-in-Waiting Su finds a way to boast about this. She finds a way to boast about everything. It's the secret of her success. Su opens her mouth to say something, and out pops something boastful.

So that's the panel. Pillars of the establishment, clearly. Hence the titles. They've volunteered their services for this urgent and unusual Ad Hoc Non-Statutory Public Inquiry because the money is excellent, and because they were invited to volunteer, and it is always flattering to be invited.

3

- Which brings us to Ozias.

Ozias has been called to the stand. Or, rather, to the hot seat. He's staying exactly where is, but the procedure is about to begin.

Is he, for example, Ozias Plume, resident of 38092 East Mulholand Drive, Hollywood, California?

Ozias says not. Or possibly not. He says it's not simple. He's currently living mostly in a hotel off Tottenham Court Road. The house on Mulholland Drive is – or was - one of his houses until recently, but he's not certain whether he still owns it.

"My affairs – rather, my *finances*," he says, "are in a bit of a mess." And then he giggles.

A visible stir in the VP Box. Gleefully, the Vested

Parties take united note. *Ozias Plumes' finances are in a bit of a mess!*

Sensible Su MBE unwraps her water glass and examines it for germs and stains. Reassured, she fills it with germ-free water, takes a couple of sips. The sound of her teeny swallows is picked up by the mic.

It echoes through the boring room, and somebody on the Everyday Benches snorts with laughter. Quickly, they look at their feet. There are security guards dotted along the walls: six of them, hands folded piously in front of groins, like teachers during school assembly. They survey the everyday people, scan them in search of the naughty snorter. But the snorter seems to have recovered. His neighbours aren't giving him away. Not for now, at least. The moment passes.

Sensible Su, feeling sufficiently hydrated, leans closer to the microphone. She scowls at Ozias, who is still giggling about his finances. "Are you telling us you have no address, Mr Plume?"

Ozias says: "Well, as I say – I'm at the hotel at the moment. Do you need me to tell you name and room number? I can, if you would like. But it seems unnecessary. I'm not sure what it's got to do with ... Also," he adds (an afterthought), "I'm not sure I want to tell you my room number."

More snorts from the everydays: three or four this time. The security guards – wagglers, all - look sharp. Abandon their groin shields and fold arms across chests. *Any more of that*, say the arms, *and it'll be straight to the headmaster's office for the lot of you.* The everydays feel it. Those that weren't giggling, tut sourly, and they all stare at their shoes. Better safe than sorry.

"… By which I mean," Ozias adds, "nothing rude or disrespectful. I just mean, being as famous as I obviously am – I don't much want to tell the whole world where I'm hunkered down… A lot of people don't like me."

Another buzz of activity from the spinners and spadders and the other note-takers. *A lot of people don't like Ozias Plume AND his finances are in a mess! (That's what happens, everyday people, when you laugh disproportionately.)*

Sensible Su shifts her body axis toward the other panellists. She motions, with a sanitised hand, for them to mute the mics.

Can we, she asks her colleagues, *in good conscience...* continue with our public inquiries if Mr Plume withholds his official address?

Mutter-mutter-mutter.

Ozias bites his cheeks to stop himself from grinning. He doesn't want to antagonise them and he's aware that laughter makes them tetchy… But he thinks it's quite funny, how solemn they're all looking, in their glass cube, discussing his lack of a house. After all, here he is in London, a city he has never much liked, somewhat roughing it (for their convenience) in room 261 Hotel Tomasino, Tottenham Court Road. What more do they want?

Which question sends his cheeks into spasms. He bites down on them harder.

"Do not laugh," he says to himself. "Do not laugh. This is serious. It is not funny."

Bite, bite.

He snorts. Can't help it. A small globule of snot flies out of his left nostril and lands on the table in front of him. Gosh, he thinks. That's gross. Lucky Debs didn't see it. He picks up his phone. It's flashing with messages incoming... lawyer, accountant, ex/wife, CoS, PA... He puts it back down again.

And he waits. They all wait. Everybody waits. Would Mr Plume's answers be considered valid without the house address? Possibly not. On the other hand, he is their star witness. If they can't question him without a house address, and if he persists in not seeming to have one, it might jeopardise the Inquiry altogether. They don't want that. Added to which, though they don't say it for fear of undermining the significance of the task ahead, it is, in many ways, a pleasant surprise – a miracle - that he's turned up today at all. He might easily not turn up tomorrow… Also, they're *here* now. Dog walkers organised, etcetera.

4

"I think we should press on," declares Lord Jeremy. "We can ascertain the legality in due course. Frankly, I don't see it being an obstacle."

"Let's press ahead," agrees Dame Davina. *"Irregularitibus non obstante."*

" - Latin," observes Lord Jeremy, slightly irritated. "Shall we begin then? I'm going to kick off with an open question. Are we all happy with that?"

"Excellent plan," says Dame Davina. "He loves the sound of his own voice. If we give him enough rope, as it were… Su? Agreed?"

"Agreed," says Su. Then, quickly, while she has the chance, "I used to speak Latin almost fluently as a kid. Unfortunately, I've forgotten most of it now."

They nod, lean forward to unmute their microphones.

"Shall we begin?" says Lord Jeremy, ready to flick the switch.

"I have a thing about languages. I'm considering taking up Mandarin, if you can believe it! At my age! So…"

"Excellent," says Lord Jeremy. "Well if he starts veering into strange tongues, which he might actually, just to confuse us…we'll know where to turn."

Dame Davina says: "I read somewhere he speaks about fifteen languages!"

Lord Jeremy nods. "He's no idiot. That's for sure. We'd be foolish to imagine this is going to be easy…"

Sensible Su wants to tell them about the time the Prime Minister of Canada once observed that she had a 'mind like a steel trap', but it's too late. The mics are on, and Lord Stevens of Dirkmass and Stirton has begun.

THE INTERROGATION

"Mr Plume," he says, "Thank you for coming here today. We are conscious that you are a busy man, with many commitments, and we are indebted to you, *most grateful*, for your generosity in finding time, in what I know is an exceptionally busy schedule, to be here with us toady. Today. To be here with us today."

Ozias doesn't reply. He tips on his chair and waits for the next bit.

Lord Stevens clears his throat. "Perhaps you would like to tell us in your own words what, *in your opinion*, was the event that was – I think you're on record as referring to the incident as a 'catalyst'?" Lord Stevens sounds as if he is mocking his star witness - already. His lips, which are thin and (Ozias notes) more bluish-grey than pink, seem to curl in a way that signals incredulity.

Luckily, it doesn't bother Ozias. Not one bit. He smiles at Lord Stevens. It's actually quite a warm smile.

This is because Ozias' smiles are always warm. He's noticed the blue-grey lips, and it's led him to imagine the blue-grey life of the man who moves them. He imagines Lord Stevens during his morning ritual, scraping off his chin bristle. Lord Stevens looking at his reflection in advance of yet another ordered day: shoring himself up to continue as per every previous one, *holding the line*, as always, keeping the fresh ideas at bay.

"Absolutely!" Ozias says. And then he laughs, which is of course taboo. "I'll definitely use my own words. Unless I can think of any others… But I suppose, once I've thought of the other words, they'll be my words too–" The idea occupies him for a millisecond. Whose words are really whose? All words are there to be called on by anyone who knows them. What did Lord Stevens mean by '*in your own words*'? He says: "I'm not sure what you mean."

"He means," says Sensible Su, who doesn't like to be sidelined, "don't use other peoples' words. Use your own."

Ozias looks at Sensible Su. *Ahhh,* he thinks. *An imbecile. This may be slow work.* He feels a little sad for her, because in the following fraction of a moment, he can see it engraved in her face: the struggle, long before laughter was frowned upon, not to be the butt of other people's (eternally incomprehensible) jokes. A flash of pain for the imbecile. "Right you are," he says. "I'll get cracking. In my own words. I presume you're asking me to tell everyone about the incident in Mexico? Is that right? The miracle in Mexico."

"I wouldn't refer to it as a miracle," snaps Lord Jeremy.

"But you mean when the guy appeared out of thin air? That's what you want me to talk about? Am I right? I don't want to waste everyone's time."

Lord Jeremy inhales. He is trying to be patient. "I would like you to describe the incident you have spoken about on numerous platforms already, during which an unknown gentleman wearing unusual garments approached you... You might begin with a timeframe. When did this alleged incident occur?"

ONLY FOUR MONTHS AGO

Only four months ago Ozias Plume was a different kind of a man. Disagreeable and unhappy. Also, lonely. At that time he employed more than 100,000 people around the globe, and trusted none of them. There was no one he much respected, almost no one he liked, and he loved not a soul in the world –

except for one. Just one. And he had lost her long ago.

Several times a year, he used to take himself off on retreats to try and catch a breather from his disdain, which was unrelenting. He longed for a simple life, or so he told himself. In California he kept a team – Team Eden: 29 strong - whose single task it was to research and facilitate this fuzzy yearning - while taking into account that, for Ozias, even the simplest life required special food from special kitchens, special mattresses from the down of special ducks; special landing pads for special helicopters, special permissions, special musicians, special beaches, special skies and special jungles... His list of simple needs grew longer every year. Ozias wasn't stupid. Far from it. He ought to have noticed this, but he did not.

Not surprisingly, the retreats always ended in failure. No matter how diligently Team Eden approached the challenge, no matter what world had been created or what crowd had been assembled to allay his unease– therapists, nutritionists, shamans, hypnotists, hookers, chefs, children, wives... Ozias would return to his California base feeling more unhappy and lonelier than ever before.

7

THE INCIDENT occurred on day three of a seven-day retreat in a Mexican jungle, his third retreat in five months. The Eden Team had cleared the beach of prickly fish and sprayed the jungle with mosquito repelling perfumes. The camp, with steam room, yoga studio and underground sound bath, had been purpose-built for his wellness, mostly out of bamboo and banana leaves. It would have been perfect, so he told himself, if he and the team hadn't organised for his American wife of almost a year, Jacinda, to be his Simple Life companion of the week.

Big mistake. It turned out, on closer examination, that she was horrid. Jacinda's sole mission in life, it occurred to Ozias on that extraordinary holiday, was to make everyone around her as miserable as she was - which, judging from her ceaseless whingeing and the sour expression on her smooth and symmetrical face, was very miserable indeed. She bitched and moaned from morning until night. Also, he realised, despite her physical perfection – no one could argue with that - she was *ugly*. Ozias realised about halfway through Day 2 that he couldn't look at his wife without feeling depressed. This was grim for both of them. But mostly, Ozias was conscious of how grim it was for him.

Anyway. After Day Two came Day Three. They

had squabbled over breakfast about the air conditioning. And then, without even discussing it with him first, Jacinda had ordered the Eden people to get her airlifted back to civilisation. She said she wanted to go shopping in Playa Norte – she *needed* to go shopping in Playa Norte. She promised she would be back in time for dinner.

"Don't bother," Ozias said, because he felt he had to say it, to save face. He didn't mean it. Of course he wanted her back for dinner. The thought of an evening alone with his teeming head, and with no one to despise but himself was - unconscionable, actually. If she wasn't back by 5.30pm he would get someone else flown in. If she wasn't back my 6.30pm he'd fucking sue for divorce. He might do it anyway. The sooner the better, for all the obvious reasons.

It meant that on Day Three, between finishing breakfast at around 8.30am, until sometime in the late afternoon, Ozias Plume almost had the day to himself.

His Chief of Staff would be present in person at 11am, for 45 minutes, and on-call, obviously, thereon in. Plus, he had the masseuse. And the sound bath therapist. But other than that...

He had decided that he might wander through the insect and snake-free undergrowth, to the beach that had been swept for spy devices and spiky fish. He was, as he reminds the panellists, 300 miles from the nearest city, surrounded by 50 miles of impenetrable, protected jungle. It ought to have been quite a nice feeling for a man on retreat from humanity, and yet-

"Are you saying," interjects Lord Jeremy, "that no one in the world, without a helicopter, could have reached the spot you were in…?"

"Yes I am!" replies Ozias, happy to have been understood. "It's exactly what I am saying."

Lord Jeremy's wooden face looks quizzical. "Really? In today's world that's quite a claim."

"That's right your Lordship!" Ozias replies. "It was the whole point. I was trying to get away from people. I was in the thick of the thick of the thickest of thick jungles…" He falls silent. With so much talk of jungles, Ozias Plume has been struck by a realisation: Lord Jeremy looks like a snake. With his piercing gaze, his yellowish skin, his slim body coiling towards the microphone, he looks, to Ozias, indistinguishable from Kaa in *The Jungle Book*.

"…Sorry," says Ozias. "What was I saying?…"

Lord Jeremy blinks. It's a slow blink, because he is, once again, trying to contain his irritation…

Trussssst in me.

His Lordship's resemblance to Kaa from *The Jungle Book* has frozen Ozias' thought processes.

Ozias can't stop staring. He mustn't say it. He mustn't say, or sing, *Trusssst in Me*. He must not tell Lord – Lord Whatsisname that he looks like

Kaa in *The Jungle Book*.

"*Sssssss-nakey…*" says Ozias instead. It slips out. He says it because it's impossible not to say something, and he's trying with all his might not to say the other thing.

Debs laughs and gulps it back. Maybe a couple of others laugh, too, quickly and quietly. But the mood in the room isn't happy: far from it. Ozias Plume is making people nervous. There is a time and a place to say *sssss-nakey*. Maybe. But this isn't it.

Behind him, in the VP Box, the spads and spods and other note-takers chunter and tut… *childish, disrespectful, hateful, elitist…* and so on.

When people ask what it is, exactly, that this Inquiry is attempting to uncover – it can be hard for the grown ups in the room to come up with an answer. But basically it's - this. Isn't it.
It's *this,* indefinable whisper of - whatever the hell it is. People saying *sssnakey.*

Ozias senses the ill will. He senses the unease and the resentment. Unfortunately, this only intensifies his urge to laugh. His body shakes. He wishes it might stop. He doesn't mean to be difficult. He's not trying to be unkind.

… But Lord Jeremy's irritation, which is quite intense, is doing something alarming to his wooden face. The skin has mottled, and his little blue eyes have shrunk. There are tiny, lumpy pouches gathering around the sides of his mouth, making him look even more like Kaa in *The Jungle Book*. Ozias Plume digs his nails into the palms of his hands, but it doesn't work. His face cracks into a massive grin.

"Have you quite finished?" His Lordship snaps.

"*Ysssssssssssssssss*," Ozias says. It slips out. And then: "Forgive me. I'm truly sorry. You're a handsome man, your Lordship. I wouldn't say it otherwise. But do you remember the snake in *The Jungle Book?*"

Dame Davina has had enough of this nonsense. "Mr Plume," she says, before his Lordship has a chance to answer. "If we could return to the matter in hand…"

"Absolutely!" Ozias says. "Yes please. I'm so sorry."

"Aside from breakfast on that particular morning, did you ingest anything at all? Were you taking any medications?"

Ozias says, "No medications. But that's a fair question."

"I'm pleased you think so," replies Dame Davina.

"No medications and not even coffee. I was on a wellness retreat, remember. The only thing I had eaten all day - or 'ingested', as you so rightly put it - was a papaya, which I had plucked that same morning from a branch that overhung my bedroom balcony. Also – a lime. There was a lime tree on the terrace. I used my penknife to cut them both open.… It was very delicious."

A surly silence from the panellists: part jealousy, part suspicion: mostly irritation. They don't believe him.

"What about water?" Dame Davina asks. "I presume you drank some water?"

Ozias smiles a little ruefully - "San Pelegrino. In those days, I was a bit paranoid. I only drank from freshly opened bottles of San Pelegrino. My team brought them in on the - you know. On the helicopter."

8

Aside from the meeting with his Chief of Staff, Ozias Plume had nothing much to do that morning. After breakfast, and with his wife gone, he found himself at a loose end. This did not happen often, and it made him anxious. He thought of spending the time on the beach, looking for turtles eggs. Studying nature. Would that get him to 11am? Possibly not. He wondered what normal people did on beaches, and he remembered the tradition for 'reading novels'. Ozias hadn't read a novel for thirty years - not since school. He tried to think of one that might interest him, but he couldn't think of any novels at all. He wanted a short novel, he told the team, to read on the beach.

Someone suggested *Animal Farm*.

"So I asked my people to bring me a copy of *Animal Farm*," Ozias tells the Inquiry. He looks at Lord Jeremy and the Dame/s-In-Waiting. "Have you read it? I mean – it's a *very* good book."

Su has a natural bent for the written word. She wants to tell the Inquiry about the time Chinua Achebe complemented her on her ear for poetic dialogue. But she bites it back. She says, *Yes! It's a marvellous book. I read it when I was eight."*

Ozias nods and smiles in sympathy. "I'm not sure I would have understood it aged eight... Maybe we're not talking about the same book? Because of course..."

Everyone waits, but it appears that Ozias has nothing more to add. He is lost in thought. Dame Davina clears her throat. "... Mr Plume?"

He says: "I wanted a physical copy. It seemed more traditional. Anyway, so they got me one... Amazingly. I always wondered if one of the team already had it with them... but it doesn't matter, does it? By lunchtime, there it was. A lovely hardback copy of *Animal Farm*, delivered to me on my lunch tray. I didn't read it, in any case. Not at that point. Things had moved on. But I just thought... We should read more novels, don't you think so?" He addresses no one and everyone. "They soothe and engage the mind in the way that nothing else really does…I mean. Apart from sex, obviously..."

At the mention of sex, Dame Davina worries that the everyday people might start giggling again. "Mr Plume," she says. "If we could stick to the topic. Is this relevant?"

Her question sets off a couple of muffled snorts. The security guards look alert.

"Relevant to what?… Yes, I think so…Watching ants around an ant hole– that's also very engaging. Very soothing. And flowers in the breeze can be captivating… Obviously butterflies…" Ozias' mind snaps back to his original point. "There are a lot of things more soothing and captivating than reading a novel, what am I talking about? On the other hand, maybe–"

Somebody at the back, a young man with a tattoo on his face, lets out an unwitting grunt. He crunches forward, puts his head in his hands. His shoulders are shaking.

Ozias swivels around, clocks the young man, glances at Debs. She grins. He grins. Then, quickly, he swivels to face front again. The tattoo man is still laughing.

Dame Davina says, with a lot of hauteur: *"I think the gentleman at the back is in need of some assistance."*

But the man keeps laughing. He's laughing too hard to offer any opposition as the security

Daisy Waugh

wagglers make their way along the bench towards him, and lift him by the armpits, and carry him from the room.

WHERE WERE WE?

A seemly pause. And then Lord Stevens of Dirkmass and Stirton grasps the metaphorical baton.

"Mr Plume," he says, "you were telling us about the hours prior to the alleged incident. So you went to the beach - *without* the novel, I take it? You had only eaten a fresh papaya, plucked directly from the tree and prepared by you, and you had ingested no medications? I take it – perhaps you might confirm – you had also taken no hallucinogens of any kind?"

"Hallucinogens?" repeats Ozias. "Certainly not! It was only nine in the morning."

"No hallucinogens to your knowledge? Within the last twenty-four hours?" amends the lord.

"No hallucinogens full stop!" Ozias replies. "You know I was tremendously fussy back then. Very conscious of my health. I had advisers– physicians, nutritionists -you name it, my Lord. They kept spreadsheets and charts. Monitored everything. It's all on record, somewhere. What went in…What came out." A schoolboy smirk. "Sorry… But you asked."

Lord Jeremy is not convinced that he did ask. Nevertheless. He's finding it hard to keep the witness on track. He refuses to be distracted by any more of Ozias' puerile red herrings.

He breathes deeply and says: "So you went to the beach, without the novel. What did you do next?"

10

As previously noted, Ozias didn't know what to do next. He went to the beach. For a few minutes he tried to look for turtle eggs but then - he didn't find any. He couldn't concentrate on turtle eggs in any case, because of the anxiety inside him, which was worse than usual because of the intense pressure he was now under to relax. The anxiety felt like maggots burrowing in his stomach. They made him want to shit. Also – more importantly – they were making him miserable.

It was too hot in Mexico. That was the chief problem. It might have been perfect, he supposed, if only there had been a breeze.

And so, Ozias Plume, the richest and possibly the loneliest man in the world, sat on the sand beneath a coconut tree, the better to hate himself.

*

"I was such a fool," he says to the panellists. "It amazes me, looking back. I almost feel sorry for myself." He laughs. It's not clear to the panel whether he is joking, or – if indeed he is joking– which part is the joke.

There he sat. At a loose end and all alone on the Mexican beach. His phone was sand proof, so he'd been told. But (he wondered) was it also sun, sea and salt-proof? No doubt Team Eden had three other sand-sea-sun-and-salt-proof devices hidden behind the banana leaves for just such an emergency. Nevertheless, the possibility of the phone in his hand potentially not functioning correctly – was an irritant. Just one more irritant for the maggots to feast on. And what if Jacinda didn't return for dinner?

To his intense relief, he thought of something to do.

He put in a call to Chak Bruton.

Nobody was quite as rich or as Google-searched as Ozias Plume, but Chak had a few billions, apparently, and the two men were of a similar age and build. Also, both had spent some formative years in Blighty, which gave them an amusing accent in common – They tended to ham it up for one another's entertainment. Neither man had ever fully grasped the concept of friendship, but they joshed together in a friend-like manner, sometimes as often as once a week.

Chak answered Ozias' call right away. He bellowed into the phone: "Ozzzziiie my old mate!

How's the Mexican jungle doing for you? Is it, in fact, one *massive* bugs'n'alligators shitbowl? I know it is. Tell me I'm right."

Ozias regretted calling him at once. He always did. This morning, Chak's awfulness jarred more than usual. Even so, it was good to hear a voice. Ozias informed Chak that the bugs had been eliminated for his visit, and that to his knowledge there were no alligators in Mexico. "I'm on a beach, looking for tortoise eggs," he said, which wasn't strictly true anymore.

Chak did a laugh. He updated Ozias on his own situation. He was in a bathtub in Hudson Yards, New York City, having his back scrubbed by a beautiful teenage girl who could not speak one word of English. "Could be worse, eh! Can't complain! Better than a turtle egg any day! Why are you calling me?"

Ozias updated him on the Jacinda situation. Turned out she was horrid, etc. etc. He was sending divorce papers this week, before the twelve-month clause kicked in.

"Right-i-ho," said Chak. But it didn't explain why Ozias was calling.

Because, Ozias said, he didn't think Jacinda would be coming back for dinner, or maybe even at all. He wondered if Chak would like to join him this evening. "I'll send the plane," he said. "Where are you?"

Chak reminded him.

"Oh yes," Ozias said. He wasn't very interested. "Come to dinner tonight. It's paradise out here. Turtle eggs. Everything. We've got everything you need. Anything else, you name it, I'll get it flown in."

Chak said howsabout flying in this bathtub, and this gorgeous girl who can't speak English?

Ozias said: "I'll get the team on it. Send me your address."

Chak had been joking. He needed to be in Miami in a couple of days in any case (or so he said.) He told Ozias that he was required at a brunch here in Hudson Yards for a couple of hours. "But worry not, my old chum. For turtle eggs you shall not search alone! I'll be with you by dinner."

That settled that. Ozias hung up feeling relieved and irritated in about equal measure. The last thing he wanted was Chak for dinner. On the other hand – at least Chak was coming for dinner. He looked at his phone. Still working. He became aware of a trickle of sweat rolling from armpit to swimming trunk waistband. *Irritating.* Took the swimming trunks off and sat on them. More comfortable. Gazed out to sea. Now what?

Then What?

Then he called his lawyers and told them to get the divorce papers ready.

Then, for no reason at all – except to spite the

manufacturers, also to irradicate the irritation of the possibility that it might not work in the sun, he tossed his phone into the sea. He watched it land in the shallow water. He watched the waves washing over it gently.

And for a moment the sight soothed him. He breathed out. No phone! He looked up through the branches of the coconut tree, noticed the big blue sky and thought: *nice*.

Not for long.

It was too hot. The team might have found him a beach with a breeze. Most beaches had breezes, in his experience. Would it have been so hard for them to find a beach with a breeze? He felt like a sausage on a grill.

At that point, he must have blinked.

11

"I must have blinked, your Lordship," Ozias tells Lord Stevens of Dirkmass and Stirton – not because he is ignoring the Dame/s-in-Waiting, but because it tickles him each time he says "Lordship." Also, he cannot remember the women's names.

Sensible Su MBE does not like to be sidelined. She says: "May I remind you, Mr Plume– to address your comments *to the panel*. There are in fact three of us sitting here."

"Of course! I'm so sorry, Madam – Mrs – Lady Panellist. When I say your Lordship, I mean also Your Ladies. Your Ladyship Panellists..."

Sensible Su MBE might have said more. For example, she might have informed Ozias that a more correct form of address would have been–

But Dame Davina is having none of it.

"Carry on," Dame Davina snaps.

"– The point is," Ozias continues, "I think I must have blinked."

"And what makes you think that?" asks Lord Jeremy, sounding sceptical and superior, as usual.

"- *Because, your Lord and Ladyships,* there I was, all alone on that big beach – and it was a big beach. I imagine you have the photograph?"

A shuffling of papers in the Panellists' Box. Yes. Of course they have the photograph. The photograph has been available on-line ever since Ozias first came up with his preposterous story. Many millions of people from all over the world have examined it, some of them very closely. There is a theory doing the rounds that the beach in the photograph – a beach to end all beaches, needless to say: a half mile or more of pure beach perfection – doesn't actually exist. Has never existed. It is nothing more than a piece of high-tech artistry: a figment of Ozias' disconcerting imagination and extraordinary occupational savvy.

Does the beach exist?

To the great bores of Twitter, formerlyknownasX, this has become a divisive question. Believing or not believing in the existence of the beach is a mark, to the other camp, of 100 per cent moral decrepitude. The end.

Anyway, Lord Stevens and the Dame/s-in-Waiting believe very much that it *does not* exist. Obviously. However, nobody in either camp seems able to settle the question once and for all. Team Eden, now disbanded, has been silent, because there is no Team Eden anymore. Its members have disappeared into the mist. They are the only ones who would know for sure, and wherever they are, they have carried the mystery with them.

In the meantime… Ozias insists that the beach in the photograph does exist, very much so, although he couldn't point to it with any confidence on a map, and furthermore –

– that it is the beach where he believes he must have blinked.

"I think you've got the photograph in front of you, have you?" Ozias asks again. "Is that what you're looking at?"

It is what they are looking at. But the panellists can't bring themselves to say so. Ozias, being very intuitive these days, understands that it's their pride which is impeding them. He looks at their dignified faces, frowning over the photograph. He imagines their orderly thighs beneath the desk, covered in blue and grey fabrics. He imagines their bottoms, flattened on their VIP seats. *Be kind,* he thinks. It would be no fun to be any one of them. So, he bites his cheeks, and talks on, without waiting for an answer.

"I was on the beach. Very hot, as I say. And naked, of course. Which was awkward." He grins. The panellists glare. In the VP Box they scribble mightily… But there are a couple of unmissable gurgles from the everyday people and on close inspection it would appear that one of the security guards is looking suspiciously hard at his feet.

It's not the thought of Ozias naked on the beach that's making them laugh, but the fury on the faces of the panellists. Ozias pushes on. He is arriving at the crux of story.

"And there he was! Out of nowhere!"

A pause.

"Who?" barks Dame Davina. "There *who* was, Mr Plume. Please be specific."

"He was standing right in front of me, smiling. This amazing smile. The sort of smile you couldn't help responding to… I was in a lousy frame of mind, as I have explained, and the next thing I knew, there was this man, appearing out of thin air, standing in front me – and we were grinning at each other without a care in the world. It was extraordinary."

"Wait a moment!" Lord Jeremy snaps. "Mr Plume. You're jumping. How are we to make sense of this account if you insist on jumping all over the place?"

Ozias is confused. "I haven't jumped," he says. "That's the whole point. He just appeared out of nowhere. Smiling. It was extraordinary."

"Yes indeed, but Lord Stevens wants to know *what* was extraordinary," says Sideline Su. "You've jumped to the point where you're telling us it was extraordinary. But - *what* was extraordinary?"

Slow Work, Be Kind.

"Well, almost everything, your Ladyship," Ozias explains. "I never smiled in those days. I certainly never smiled at strangers appearing out of nowhere, and definitely not when I was paying through the nose to be in the middle of the jungle on a very private retreat. Normally I would have been infuriated. *Who the fuck is this man, appearing out of nowhere?* That sort of thing. You have to understand – aside from my own longing for privacy, there were security questions. This guy might have been smiling his lovely smile, but for all I knew he might have wanted to kill me. A lot of people did back then. So – My Lord. And My Ladies. Everything was extraordinary about the situation. His appearance out of nowhere was extraordinary; his peculiar clothes, his lovely face, his beautiful smile. And then *me* - the most irritable man in the world, sitting there, naked, smiling back at him. It was *all* extraordinary."

12

"You seem to imply that you weren't afraid," says Lord Jeremy, who is used to thinking he's the cleverest chap in the room. "It's rather hard to believe…" He smirks. "As you rightly point out. There are a lot of people out there who want to kill you."

Ozias says: "Not so many anymore, of course…"

"Oh, I wouldn't be too sure about that," fires back Lord Jeremy. A scattering of titters from the adults in the room. (Some laughter is still funny.)

Ozias gazes at the lord. He notes the laughter. He doesn't want to insult the panellists by stating the obvious. He doesn't want to be rude. On the other hand, maybe they genuinely haven't understood? He says: "It's just the maths, your Lordship. I have many more friends now. Millions and millions of friends! There are so many of us now… In a roundabout way it's why I'm sitting here, isn't it?"

"You vastly overestimate your importance, Mr Plume," says Lord Jeremy.

"We are here," Dame Davina sneers, "not to examine your friendship groups, Mr Plume, but to put some of your increasingly nonsensical, dangerous and unscientific claims under a little forensic light."

Ozias shrugs. "I'm just pointing out –"

"–If you please, Mr Plume," interrupts Lord Jeremy, who is in danger of blowing his top. "I must insist that you stick to the topic."

Ozias laughs. He laughs with gusto. "If you don't mind my saying, your Lordship, I'm trying my best to stick to the topic, but your Lord and Ladyships keep butting in with unnecessary questions…I think it's because you're nervous of what I might be going to say. Is that possible?" He's teasing them. "I'm not sure what you expected from me. After all, you invited me here to say it!"

Dame Davina takes a deep breath. Her deep voice drops another couple of notes, and she speaks very slowly: "Mr Plume, we would like you to tell us about the morning on the beach in Mexico. I'm sorry if this request confuses you. When you're ready, please continue."

Ozias smiles at her. He tries again. "So, this amazing guy appeared out of nowhere–"

"We'll return to the manner in which he 'appeared', in due course," [Lord Jeremy. He can't stop himself.] "Of course he didn't appear 'out of nowhere'. That's not a realistic explanation. We will assume that he appeared from behind the trees while you were on the telephone to Mr Bruton. Would you like to describe this 'smiling gentleman' for us please? What was he wearing?"

Ozias says: "But the trees were behind me. I was looking out towards the sea. I was looking at the spot where the mobile had plopped into the water. And then I blinked. And really, you know, I'm only saying I blinked for… dramatic effect. I didn't blink. Or if I did blink I blinked the way we all blink. Which – I've googled it – takes approximately 1/3 of a second."

"You may have had some sand in your eye," offers Sensible Su. "That might be an explanation. You were on a sandy beach, after all. In my experience, a blink can last much longer when the eyes are exposed to bright sunshine, for example, or if you're on a windy beach. Or a mosquito or a small grain of sand lands unexpectedly in the eyes. One can blink for several moments at a time."

Ozias lets this float. There doesn't seem to him to be much point in responding to it. Su gazes down at him earnestly, keen to have these possibilities acknowledged: and a short silence falls. It highlights the muffled giggle from the Everyday Benches. Hearing it, Ozias' cheek muscles kick into action again. He notes they have a will of their own.

He talks quickly, to cover it: "He was wearing colourful shorts. Rainbow coloured shorts. Very baggy. And a heavily embroidered coat or long jacket, a bit like a Royal courtier. Gilt tassels. Gold buttons. It was red. Very, very bright red, and it was open at the front. His chest was brown and smooth and very shiny. Obviously, he was sweating…" Ozias pauses.

"… Any other details spring to mind?" Lord Jeremy asks, in that sardonic way of his.

"Yes," says Ozias. "*Lots.* He had a long, grey beard. Like Moses." Once again, he pauses. "… And there was some foliage caught up in it. Little twigs. And he had beautiful golden hair."

"My goodness," says Su, uncertainly. "… How gorgeous!"

"A halo of golden curls and a grey beard with twigs in it?" Lord Jeremy repeats.

Ozias nods. "That's quite right, your lordship. And a very shiny face. He looked young and old. Dark and blonde. And on his head, he was wearing a riding hat."

Silence.

What to do with that?

Dame Davina and Lord Jeremy feel bubbles of rage fizzing around their windpipes and oesophageal sphincters. Ozias Plume, it occurs to them, is making things up as he goes along! He's *mocking* them!

In a playground, back in the olden days, they might have come up behind him and given him a good thump. It would have wiped the shiny smirk off his face.

But this is now. It's not how they operate. Also, they are separated by thick panes of glass and several meters of flooring.

Lord Jeremy prepares to take control. He's about to say: "Mr Plume, I don't believe you. I think you're making things up as you go along. I think you have come up with that description off the top of your head because you want to make a mockery of this Inquiry, and I assure you…" but he hasn't yet worked out what it is he's about to assure: what threat he can make Ozias Plume that would have the slightest effect on him. So – there's a micro-second of hesitation, and into it slips Sensible Su.

"The rainbow shorts are very interesting," she observes.

Ozias says: "Thank you."

"He was wearing shorts in the colours of the rainbow? Did I hear that correctly?" she asks, growing in confidence.

"Yes," Ozias replies. "You heard that correctly."

"So we can presume that he was a progressive and sensible man, in touch with modern sentiment. Would that be a fair assumption Mr Plume?"

Ozias stares at her. "I have no idea if that is a fair assumption, and I'm not completely sure how it's relevant… It wasn't really a political moment…"

"Hmmm," she says, into her microphone, and scribbles something onto her notes. What she scribbles is:

Rainbow rainbow

And then she underlines it.

Dame Davina cuts in. "Let's leave the physical description for now. Let's move on. Would you like to tell us what occurred during this fabled encounter, according to your memory? How long did the encounter last?"

Ozias says: "I've honestly no idea. Time stood still. When he arrived, the sun was high in the sky, and when he left, the sun was high in the sky. The only difference – the only measurable difference – was my thirst. I'd not been aware of feeling thirsty before he appeared. After he left, I was parched. I would have gulped a whole litre of water! So – it might have been a few seconds. It might have been an hour…"

Dame Davina heaves an irritable sigh. It gusts across her microphone, as intended. She says: "All right. Never mind how long it lasted. What did you say to each other?"

"Ahhh!" replies Ozias, rubbing his hands together. "We arrive at last!"

13

"He was the first to speak. As far as I remember, he simply said, 'Hello.'"

"Not *'¡hola!'?*" slips in Su. She writes a note.

"- But he said it as if we were neighbours and we

Daisy Waugh

were bumping into each other at a train station or something..." (It is a long time since Ozias Plume has needed to stand at a train station.) "He said: 'Hello,' and then he said, 'Ozias Plume.' It wasn't a question. It was a statement. He told me his name was Octavius. And by the way, I don't believe it *was* his name. Because afterwards – when I was trying to find him again- absolutely –I mean, the name was no help whatsoever."

"Perhaps he didn't want you to find him?" suggests Dame Davina. Only for the sake of interrupting him. She can't actually stand it when he speaks.

Ozias smiles. "He definitely didn't want me to find him, Lady Panellist. Anyway, after he'd told me his fake name – his first fake name - very shortly after that - he stopped speaking, and he scanned me from top to toe. This was very intense. I was naked, you remember. And this was weird – obviously. But what I want you to understand is that it felt normal. Like the most normal thing. I wasn't embarrassed–"

"Were you aroused, Mr Plume?" (This from Lord Jeremy. It is meant to discombobulate the witness, but it is Lord Jeremy who finds himself blushing.)

Ozias says: "Not at all. He was looking me up and down in a very businesslike way. I had a small cut on my knee. Not very interesting. Or I wouldn't have thought so. But he stared at this cut and *then* –

this was when he produced the thing from his hand. *There it was*. In his hand. So, I suppose I have to say it must have been there all along. In my opinion, though, he simply held out his hand and then the object appeared. The jar. Like magic. In a flash. There it *wasn't* and then there it *was…*"

Su says: "Unless of course he was carrying the object – the jar - in the pocket of the coat? A disguised pocket perhaps?"

"Good point," Ozias replies, noting her lack of hostility. "*Very* good point, my Lady. He may well have been carrying it in a disguised pocket."

Su smiles. "But carry on," she says, glowing a little bit: tempted, at this point, to update everyone on the evening Stella McCartney complimented her on her 'unique interpretation of "formal dress".' "After he had presented the jar, probably from a hidden pocket, how did you react? Where was your security team?"

"My security team was nowhere to be seen."

Dame Davina leans into the mic. "So they didn't appear on the beach?" she asks, "Not at any point?"

"That's right, Lady Panellist," Ozias agrees.

"So – just to be clear," Dame Davina says, "Did anyone else appear on the beach, at any point, during this encounter?"

"No one, Madame," Ozias says.

"No one at all?"

"That's right!"

"No other witnesses whatsoever? No one else caught a glimpse of this peculiar gentleman calling himself Octavius?"

"Again," replies Ozias, beaming now, "you are quite correct! Thank you. I am grateful to you for being such an excellent listener."

He's teasing her.

Debs knows it. Her cheeks are spasming. The security guard who'd previously been looking with such suspect intensity at his feet, he knows it too. He rocks this way and that and pinches the skin on the back of one hand. It does not do the trick. With a dreadful splutter, only magnified by his efforts to supress it, he scuttles for the nearest exit.

Never to return.

In the meantime, Ozias is talking again. He wants to tell everyone about the jar and the cut on his leg. But the panellists keep interrupting with pointless questions. Not so much Lord Jeremy, to be fair. He hasn't fully recovered his embarrassment re. the matter of Ozias' arousal/lack of. But Dame Davina wants to pick holes in everything he says. And Sideline Su, as always, just likes to be heard. For some reason she's got stuck on the mystery man's provenance

"He spoke very good English," Ozias is saying, for the fourth time. "But, as I say, there was an accent. Unfortunately, as I say, I can't tell you where it was from. As I say, it was a mixture of everything. It seemed to slip and slide all over the place. All over the globe. I kept meaning to ask him, *where are you from*, Ferdinand?"

"Ferdinand?" cried Dame Davina. "I thought you said his name was–"

"Octavius. It was. But he changed it. I'll get to that. The point is there were so many questions I might have asked him –I just didn't think of them until after he'd gone."

Ozias notes the frustration inside the glass box.

He says: "I agree with you, my Lord and Lady Panellists! Very, very frustrating. So many questions left unanswered, and now here we are..."

A moment of silence.

And then another.

It is broken by a voice from the back, which shouts out quite suddenly: "CIVILISATION IS ON THE BRINK!" Seven or eight people laugh, including Ozias.

Dame Davina smacks her hand on the panellist counter (this not being a gavel-using scenario). The noise cuts through the laughter. It's quite shocking. She calls for silence and then waits as the laughter settles down, and a pair of security wagglers step forward to escort the voice from the back off the premises.

The person whose voice it is, has to be lifted from his seat and carried, just like the previous one. He too cannot stop laughing. His entire face is creased, his eyes are screwed so tight he can't see, and there are tears on his cheeks.

"Ohhh," he gasps, "easy does it! Let me down!" But he's giggling so much that nothing matters: least of all, *civilisation on the brink.* The wagglers look stern. Dame Davina looks savage, Sideline Su looks traumatised, and Lord Jeremy finds, at last, that he can move on from his embarrassment re. Ozias' penis. Lord Jeremy watches the scene unfold and he thinks:

The situation might be worse than we realise.

Dame Davina's rage is, of course, fuelled by a similar sense of foreboding. "Any more of this," she declares, "… from *anyone…* and I will personally see to it that you are charged under Section Xc1 of the Hateful and Hurtful Misconduct Act, for which – I would remind you, there is a maximum custodial sentence of…" she glances at Lord Jeremy.

"Eighteen years," he says.

"Eighteen years," she reiterates.

"Please, people, settle down," pleads Sensible Su. She suggests that it might be a good time to break for lunch.

"Good idea," says Ozias. "I think maybe we're all feeling a bit peckish."

14

Lunch happens.

Ozias and Debs stay on the premises. They sit on a bench round the corner from the main corridor, outside the disabled toilets, and eat tuna and raw onion sandwiches which they made together in Deb's mother's campervan yesterday evening. They discuss the sandwiches as they eat them. Debs wonders if they might have been improved with coriander.

Ozias says: "I don't think this sandwich could be improved in any way."

And then Debs says: "I agree with you. But I think the raw onions were a mistake."

Ozias chortles. "And *yet*," he says, with his mouth full. He air-kisses his fingertips, to denote the sandwich's perfection.

"And *yet*," agrees Debs. A bread crumb goes flying.

They both find this incredibly funny.

And then the bell rings and they have to file back into the boring room to continue with the hostile questioning.

15

Lord Jeremy waits until people are settled. He clears his throat. He says: "Mr Plume, when you are ready, please continue… The panellists have agreed over lunch that we must allow you to speak, as far as possible, without interruption. This morning, we didn't make as much progress as we had hoped. So. Without further ado…" He glances around the boring room: confers on its citizens one of his most miserly smiles… "I'm going to give you the floor, Mr Plume. Over to you!"

"Right you are," says Ozias Plume. "Very good. I think we'd got to the bit about the jar, which is probably the most important bit. So there Octavius was, in his funny clothes, and there was me, smiling away but with no swimming trunks on. And in his hand there appeared this jar: a very normal sort of a jam jar, made of glass. It had a gel-like substance inside, which was cloudy and brownish. The jar didn't have a label of any kind, and it was about ¾ full. He – I'm going to call him Octavius for the sake of argument - Octavius told me that the lotion would cure the cut on my knee… I mentioned the cut before lunch, right?"

The panellists' faces are set to look sceptical and unthreatened. This is the tactic they have agreed upon over lunch. They double down on it now. They pucker and smirk and tip their heads, and say not a word.

Ozias grins.

Finally, Lord Jeremy says: "Yes indeed. You mentioned 'the cut'. Please continue."

"Anyway – the cut was nothing. As I said, I don't

even remember how I came by it. Ok so the point is, *as he was looking at my knee* it began to throb! The cut began to throb! It was as if his eyes were doing something to my knee just by looking at it, because the cut, which as I say I had barely noticed before, was suddenly swollen and hot. Ferdinand asked me what I had done to my knee, and I said, '*Nothing.* It's just a scratch.'… But he kept on gazing at the cut, and the more he gazed the sorer it became, until the wound literally broke open, and there was blood pouring down my shin… and I was in a great deal of pain… Well, anyway – I don't know how long we watched this happening, but eventually I had to ask him to stop looking at the damn cut, because it was now quite clear that by looking at it, he was making it worse. I said to him – '*I* didn't do anything to my knee. What are *you* doing to it?' Which was a very fair question under the circumstances. But he laughed. And I have to emphasise, because I can appreciate that this sounds crazy – that while this was going on I was in really *quite excruciating* pain, and yet - as the situation continued *there was never at any point anything surprising about it.* In fact, the only time the situation ever strikes me as surprising is when I'm telling the story to others, and I see their faces..."

Cue for more smirks and grimaces from the glass box.

Ozias doesn't mind. He ploughs on. "Anyway, so he laughed. He stopped staring at the knee and stared into my eyes instead. He was holding out this jar and he said I should put some of the gel-like lotion on the wound. He said something about cuts going sceptic in the jungle, which of course everyone knows. And then he pushed this lotion at me. He'd already taken the lid off, I suppose. He wiggled the jar under my nose. He was getting impatient. He told me to hurry up…"

A pause.

"… Which is *not normal* – you understand? People didn't generally tell me to hurry up. It wasn't the… interpersonal dynamic… [he grins] I was accustomed to… I took the jar from him. It didn't look great: dried out round the rim; kind of dirty. I smelled it… I was in a lot of pain, but I didn't want to put it on my cut. In those days I must have spent several millions a year on doctors and nutritionists and all that crap... The idea that *in a million years* I might want to smear onto an open wound some filthy looking lotion given to me by a madman on a beach, out of a dirty jam jar, was… I actually cannot emphasise to you the unlikeliness of this scenario... But anyway, that's what I did.

"It smelled of mushrooms… Or maybe it smelled of lavender..." He frowns, confused. "The smell was always changing. I don't remember what it smelled like. I can never remember…"

Somebody in the Panellists' Box snorts: a dismissive type of snort, potentially cruel, disproportionate and harmful and yet not eligible for a fine in this instance.

Ozias doesn't care. "Octavius was getting impatient. There was a vibe coming off his shiny skin - visible - like heat waves, rising. And I had a strong sense that he wasn't going to hang around for me to think about it. He was on the point of vanishing again. And I knew I didn't want him to vanish because…"

Ozias thinks about this.

"Because… because… because – even when he was making my knee throb, it was *really, really nice* having him around. I loved him! Lord and Lady Panellists, I see your expressions, and believe me, I understand that this may be difficult for you to take at face value, but I could hear his heart beating and – I could feel my own heart expanding… it was glowing with this most amazing sense of… *joy*. It was… It was like nothing I ever felt before.

"So I stuck a finger in the lotion and put the lotion on the cut. And the cut was throbbing and seeping puss at this point: and blood too, but mostly puss. It was throbbing. And then –

Pouff!

A long pause. Very long. Twenty seconds for the word to land, and still nothing.

Sensible Su is the first to yield.

"*Pouff*?" she repeats. "Pouff, *what*?"

Ozias says: "Pouff, it healed. The pain stopped. The throbbing stopped. The puss and blood stopped. The cut closed up. The blood and puss dried and peeled and turned into little dust particles. And *pouff!* All sign of it was gone. It was as if nothing had ever even been there."

Ozias falls silent. It appears that, for the moment at least, he has nothing more to add. He sits bolt upright and looks around the boring room. His eyes are wide with the wonder of the thing. And he's wondering, too, now that he's told everyone the best bit, where he might see this reflected.

Not in the Panellist Box, clearly. They are looking slightly demented, Ozias thinks. But on the public benches perhaps? Or among the security wagglers standing guard by the doors? Or maybe even in the VP Box behind him, given the sardine situation? There are so many in there, maybe one among them?

The panellists say not a word. Part of their policy (agreed over lunch) is to *leave long silences* after Ozias' more preposterous claims, specifically so that their absurdity can infuse the room.

Ozias swivels this way and that, smiling widely. No one, except Debs, wants to catch his eye. As the silence extends, there comes a female voice from the VP (Vested Party) Box at the back of the room.

Her words are muffled by the glass, but the other sardines are all looking at her. She appears to be laughing, which is against the rules; except it's not the sort of laughter that's harmful, according to the unofficial criteria, because it isn't heartfelt. Ozias, being so intuitive these days, can sense this at once. In any case, whatever it is she said has set her box-mates nodding and smiling in agreement.

Ozias watches them. He turns back to the panellists. "They're smiling because they don't believe me," he says. He thinks about it. "…Or maybe they don't want to believe me? I don't know. Anyway-" He dismisses the question. "To go back to my story – that was pretty much it! End of Chapter One. When I looked up from the cut on my knee, he was gone. Vanished. He had disappeared just as he had appeared. Out of thin air. Like magic… I didn't see him again for some time."

Ozias doesn't feel like checking the room for reactions this time. He has understood that in these circumstances, the reactions are… tragic and comic in about equal measure. Comi-trag. Tragi-com. He smiles. "Obviously," he adds, "he left me with the jam jar. If he hadn't left the jam jar I would have assumed it was all a dream – including the cut, because I don't remember how I got the cut… Or even, to be honest with you, whether I even had a cut in the first place at all. But *he left the jar.* You see? And because he left the jar, I knew it was real.

I was desperate to find him again." Ozias considers this. "As you can imagine," he adds, "I was very, very accustomed to getting what I wanted."

CHAPTER TWO IN THE STORY

Ozias felt peculiar.

There he sat, alone on the beach. Still naked. Still with his mobile in the sea. Hotter than he had ever been. Very, very hot. What the fuck had just happened?

He blinked. (He undoubtedly blinked.)

He looked at his knees. He thought one might be shinier than the other. Apart from that, they looked the same... More or less the same. There was a sense of wellbeing in the shiny knee, he felt: hard to define, but – most assuredly so. A meter away, lying on its side and just beyond his reach, there lay a jam jar three-quarters filled with a glutinous substance, semi-opaque and dirty brown.

He picked it up. Smelled it. It smelled of lovage.

An hour or two later, he was joined by George Houseman, his Chief of Staff, who was embarrassed to find his boss wearing no swimming trunks. There were documents to sign, litigations to initiate, decisions to be made, staff, associates, populations and governments to fuck over. *Stuff to do*. And now here was Ozias Plume, fully naked, beaming at him, and with a dirty jam jar in his hand. It was terrifying.

"George!" Ozias cried. He stood up, with his penis and everything, and he wrapped his sweaty arms around George's shoulders. "Holy *cow,* am I pleased to see you!"

George was wearing chino shorts and a t-shirt with collar; his uniform when visiting Ozias on retreats. He felt he should stand very still until the embrace was over, but he felt quite sick. He was carrying a case with iPad and mobile. He held it tight against his thighs and genital area and waited for the moment to pass.

It passed. Ozias picked up the vibe. Actually, it hit him like a thunderbolt. He released his Chief of Staff at once and apologised for having invaded his space.

"Are you all right?" George asked him. "You're – why are you naked?"

"Oh," said Ozias, glancing down at his body. "I'm so sorry. I was hot. I'll put my trunks on."

George said: "Are you all right, Ozias?"

Ozias, penis tucked safely away now, assured his Chief of Staff that he'd never felt better. "Tell me George… Be honest with me. Do my knees look funny?"

George stared at Ozias' knees for some time. He said: "They look pretty normal to me… Although that one looks… a bit shiny. Why is your knee so shiny?"

"It *is* shiny, isn't it!" Ozias sounded triumphant. "I thought I'd imagined it. I thought I might be going mad. But if it looks shiny to you, too, George, then – I have to tell you *the most extraordinary thing has just happened to me…"*

There was work to be done. Once Ozias had finished relating his preposterous story, and George had sounded the appropriate astonishment, they agreed – rather, George politely insisted - that they return to the banana leaf dining room, where they might focus better with the benefit of the air conditioning.

"Air conditioning?" Ozias repeated, holding tight to the jam jar. "Wouldn't you prefer a quick swim? I think I would."

George would have loved a quick swim. He was very hot, and the sea was sparkling blue. But there was work to be done, and also– everything about the situation was weird. Why would Ozias give a fuck if he wanted a swim? Why did Ozias keep smiling? Since when had he ever apologised?

George looked uncertain. Ozias noted this. He realised George was feeling insecure and it made his heart ache. He wanted the best for George.

He said: "Not to worry! You're probably in a hurry. Let's go in. Maybe someone could bring us some coconut water. Would you like some coconut water, George?"

George said he would love some coconut water,

and they trudged across the burning sand, George clutching his electronic work gadgets, Ozias clutching his dirty jar, back to the banana hut.

An attendant welcomed them in. Ozias asked for coconut water and led George to the dining room, where they sat down at a table, comfortably opposite one another, just as they had a thousand times before; only this time it did not feel like business as usual, not to either of them. Ozias was preoccupied with the springiness in his shiny knee. George, after everything, and with the memory of Ozias' penis pressed against his briefcase, was one hundred per cent out of sorts.

George said: "Ahhh. Lovely and cool in here."

Ozias agreed that it was cool, but he wasn't convinced of its loveliness: "Feels a bit odd, doesn't it? Perhaps we should switch off the air con? There's something unnatural about feeling so cool in the middle of this heat."

George was an American. To him, air conditioning was fully the most natural thing in the world. Nevertheless, Ozias was his lord. So he said *yes, yes, absolutely. How right you are. Very bad for the environment, too. Perhaps we should get it turned off? Shall I go and...?"*

"No, no!" Ozias stood. He shunted the jam jar further into the middle of the table, closer to George. Paused to consider it. Confirmed, internally, that the idea was a good one, and stepped back. He said he needed a pee, anyway.

He left George Houseman alone with the jar.

It might have been enough. Ozias stopped at the doorway to check. George was staring at the jar, just as Ozias had hoped. But then George noticed Ozias noticing him staring at the jar, and he gave a jittery sort of a laugh, as if he'd been caught doing something he shouldn't.

But Ozias *wanted* him to stare at the jar! He said, "Seriously, George, have you got any aches and pains?"

"What?" replied George, burning with embarrassment. "No! Absolutely not!"

Ozias giggled, which took them both by surprise. "What, none at all? A man of your age? No backache? No… what-do-they-call-it? Mental health issues? Erectile disfunctions–"

"What?"

"No cuts or blemishes?"

"What are you talking about?"

"Nothing wrong with you at all? I thought I noticed a slight limp, coming back from the beach. A squeakiness in the hips… Or maybe you have a headache?"

"I don't have a…" George Houseman, in his embarrassment, put a finger to his forehead, and as he did so, at that very point of contact, he felt the most tremendous explosion: a most excruciating stab of pain. He yelped.

And then it was gone.

"… I don't have a headache," he finished, but with less conviction than he'd begun. "And what do you mean, a *man of my age?"* He added, trying to sound normal, like a middle-aged man at a drinks party, being jovial. "I'm not that old! My goodness, Ozias, I'm only 63!"

Ozias shrugged. "Well anyway – I'm just saying." He nodded at the jar. "Feel free to have a go… Go ahead and smear some on. I'm fascinated to know if it has the same effect on you. Or, you know, if I'm just going mad."

Ozias wandered off. And it must have been one hell of a long pee (thought George Houseman). He didn't return for ages, by which time George had done his best to put the wretched lotion, and his newly idiotic master, out of his mind. He'd fired up his electronics and was casting a chilly but expert eye over documents pertaining to the acquisition of a 1/4million hectare plot in Southern Ecuador. He had forgotten about the jam jar by the time Ozias pottered back in.

Ozias said: "Sooooooo…" He was holding an orange, chucking it up in the air and catching it, "Whassup? Did you have a go with the-" Ozias nodded at the jar.

But he could see at once that it hadn't moved. "Oh *George.* What an old stick you are! Are you telling me I left you all alone with a jar of magic, and you spent the time staring at a computer?!" Ozias belly laughed. It made the banana leaves shake. It made George jump. Actually, it gave Ozias quite a fright, too. He'd not laughed so heartfully in years. Ever. He'd not laughed so heartfully in his life before.

George decided to ignore it. As far as he was aware, the helicopter would be ready and waiting to scoop him out of this madhouse in less than forty minutes. Ozias might want to chuck oranges, and jabber about magic potions, but he rarely – never – allowed George to run over their allotted time together, and there was much to be discussed.

He said: 'Regarding the land purchase. I've had a glance at Trijborn Hetvarn's SCK input – have you seen it? I'm thinking, possibly, we can–' but as he spoke, the stabbing pain in his temple returned. It returned with such a vengeance that he had to stop talking. He inhaled sharply, put a hand to his head.

Ozias frowned. "Are you all right?"

"I'm fine! Sorry. I just… err…" But the pain was not going away. Far from it. And when George removed his hand and attempted to continue with the conversation about Trijborn's input, his hand was soaking wet. "What the…?" muttered George. And it was sticky.

Ozias stared at George. George's left temple had swollen beneath the fingertips. It was swelling more, even as Ozias watched. Beneath the skin, a smooth bump was expanding – now the size of a pea, now the size of a large marble; and now the size of a ping pong ball. "Holy cow!" cried Ozias, transfixed. "George it's going to explode! What the hell –?" Brainwave. Or not even, actually: the action was a reflex, circumventing his amazing brain. Ozias had already leaned into the middle of the table and pushed the jam jar towards George. It slid fast across the table, smacking into George's iPad.

"Hurry," Ozias ordered him. "Hurry up! Put it on before your whole head explodes."

George hesitated – but not for long. The pain was excruciating. The swelling was big enough now that its underbelly was beginning to obscure his upper peripheral vision. Also, Ozias sounded so authoritative. So certain.

"DO IT!" Ozias bellowed.

And so he did.

17

In yet another surprise turn of events, Jacinda Plume returned from her shopping trip. Ozias was lying in a hammock on the upstairs veranda, fast asleep. She glanced at him, pleased not to have to engage. She dumped her shopping on the bed and took a shower. She had a lot on her mind.

There was no wall between bedroom and

veranda; and only a cute bamboo hint of a partition between the bedroom and her shower. She glanced at Ozias, sleeping peacefully, with his mouth slightly open. She thought, maybe, that it might be in her interests to suggest they have sex. But then he snored – it was only a mini-grunt. Nevertheless. She realised she couldn't face it. Her thoughts, which were generally negative, moved on to other matters.

Chak had messaged to warn her he was in-coming.

So *that* would be interesting.

She and Chak had a flirtation going. They'd also had sex together, but that was some years ago now: 'B.O.' (before Ozias*)*, as Jacinda referred to those halcyon days, and in all honesty neither could remember much about it. Ozias, of course, was clueless.

Anyway, so Chak was incoming. She wasn't displeased with the news. It took the pressure off a bit. As a rule, she tried to avoid evenings alone with Ozias. This was easy enough - except when he plonked himself into these silly jungle retreats and insisted she come along.

She gazed at him over the bamboo partition, feeling ungenerous and mildly repulsed. Her attention was caught by movement in the distance, on the beach beyond: a male figure, dressed in his underpants. White, slimmish, middle-aged. He was trying to climb into a hammock, by the looks of it; raising one foot toward the rope netting, wobbling, losing his nerve, snatching it back again. She frowned. What the-

She grabbed a towel.

"Ozias? Ozias! Ozzie wake up!"

His eyes sprung open. "Hello, my darling!" he said.

She stood in front of him, scowling, dripping in water. Utterly beautiful, of course, in a way. He smiled at her. A lovely, warm smile. He said: "What a wonderful surprise."

" - What?"

"I didn't think you would be back so soon. Actually, I wasn't certain you'd be back at all."

She paused, not sure if he was being sarcastic. She said: "Ozias, what is George Houseman doing in his underpants, down there on the beach?"

"Hmm? Oh, *George*... He told me he'd never slept under the stars. Never slept in anything but a bed. Not once, in 63 years!" Ozias shook his head. He chuckled. "Poor devil! What a life, eh? Can you believe that?"

She stared at Ozias.

"I get the impression," observed Ozias, watching fondly as Houseman's hammock struggles played on, "that he's settling in for the night... Look at him!" Ozias laughed, yet again: a big, happy laugh. "He's frightened of falling on the sand! Only imagine how the stars are going to terrify him!"

She shrugged, fully flummoxed. "…So what?"

Ozias said, "By the way Chak's coming in. You like Chak, don't you? I wouldn't have asked him if I knew you were coming back… but I thought I'd pissed you off so much this morning…" Another smile. Another moment involving warm eye contact.

Jacinda could bear it no longer. She turned away, muttering about the evening being spoilt, pretending she'd been really looking forward to spending an evening *à deux*. Ozias ignored this. Maybe he didn't hear her. He stood up and stretched. He needed to say something urgent to George about the Ecuadorian hectares. He'd had a brainwave. He'd never met any Ecuadorians, but he imagined, correctly, that his brainwave would make them very happy.

18

George didn't want to join the others for dinner. Neither did Ozias, but he was conscious that Chak had come all the way from – somewhere (he couldn't remember), and that really it would be disrespectful to spend the whole night ignoring him, giggling on the beach with George.

So Chak, Jacinda and he sat down at the bamboo dining table. Very rustic. There was a wholesome feast prepared, a separate one for each for them, taking into account their specific requirements: too detailed to list.

In any case, Ozias wasn't hungry. Earlier, he and George had tramped out into the jungle – they'd gone way off piste – and stuffed their chops with miniature bananas. He sat at the dining table for a while, watching Jacinda and Chak nibbling from their individual troughs. He was feeling a bit dazed. But they seemed, he thought, to have the conversation in hand. They seemed to be getting on well. He thought Jacinda looked a bit strange, and couldn't work out why, until he realised it was unusual to see her smiling.

Chak said: "You're a bit quiet, old chum. What happened? Did the turtles eat your tongue?"

It made Jacinda laugh.

"No, no," Ozias assured him. "I haven't found any turtles yet. I just ate a lot of bananas."

Chak, raising his glass, as if making a toast, said to Ozias: "Beware the bananas," which meant nothing whatsoever, but it made Jacinda laugh, yet again.

"No – actually," said Ozias, "I was just thinking how lovely you both looked when you laughed."

Yikes.

A silence. And not a happy one.

Finally Chak said: "I've got the vomit emoji in my head. I'm putting it out there. Slapping that emoji on the table right now. Ozias, what the fuck is the matter with you? Snap out of it, old man. You're giving me the creeps."

Jacinda was staring at him. Perhaps she was looking at him properly for the first time since the shower, when he was snoring, and she was feeling repulsed. She said: "Ozzie – have you looked in the mirror? Why is your face so shiny?"

Ozias leaned forward, alert and engaged again. "Is it?" he said. "That's what George said before dinner. I can't see it. But the thing is, George's face is shiny too. Really shiny. It looks like he's glowing. Like an angel. Do I look like I'm glowing? I feel as if I'm glowing… Guys – *the most extraordinary thing happened to me this afternoon…*"

They didn't believe him. He went upstairs to his bedside table to fetch the old jam jar. He placed it onto the table between them and waited for something to happen. But nothing happened. No weeping cuts, no exploding boils. Nothing. Jacinda and Chak looked from Ozias to the jam jar and back again.

Chak said. "I think we need to call the doc. You've obviously got sunstroke."

"I haven't got sunstroke. I've got a shiny face. And I feel fantastic. And so does George. Ask him. I'm just saying – you've got nothing to lose. If you want a shiny – Jacinda, come on, I know how much you care about your skin, and I respect you for that… Well… I don't know if I respect you for that... I don't feel either way about it. But if you want a shiny face and you want to feel fantastic… *try it.* Go on! *Try it."*

It was a non-starter.

Ozias took back the jar. 'Well," he said, giving up. "I'm going with George to have a look for the turtles. Want to come?"

Jacinda said she was tired. Chak said he would keep Jacinda company. Ozias, standing up, clutching the jar, noticed the vibe passing between them. It was big. They couldn't wait for him to be gone.

He thought: *ahh well.*

He said: "You guys have fun. And if you change your mind about my lotion… just give me a shout."

He pottered off.

DAY TWO OF THE PUBLIC INQUIRY

It starts badly. It starts especially badly for Dame Davina, whose driver arrives at her house 35 minutes late.

She is vile, in her smartarse fashion, when he finally turns up. She can hardly look at him - which is fortunate because he can't stop smiling. The more brusque and self-important she becomes, the harder he finds it to keep a straight face. She wants to know – repeatedly – why he has arrived at her house thirty-five minutes late, and whether he is in the habit of arriving at clients' houses thirty-five minutes late, when they have been booked to arrive thirty-five minutes earlier.

"Is it normal practice to arrive thirty-five minutes late, in your experience? Is that normal practice? I imagine if it were, you wouldn't have many clients left, now would you?"

He is late, he explains, because the office computer sent him to the wrong pick-up address. Dame Davina *doubts that very much.*

But it so happens it's true. This morning a lot of the drivers have been sent the wrong pick-up addresses.

In any case, he apologises and spends the rest of the journey biting back his giggles. Dame Davina has typewritten notes on her lap – but she can't concentrate on them: she's too angry. Each time the driver catches her angry face in the rear-view mirror, he feels a pang: a complicated mix of hilarity and sorrow. *Poor, miserable old thing*, he thinks.

After the initial exchanges they travel mostly in silence – until, through the haze of her fury, she notices something else to be angry about.

She says: "For crying out loud. What's wrong with the traffic lights?"

The driver bites his shiny cheeks and says: "I

don't know, Madame. It's a mystery. There's been a lot of confusion this morning."

Dame Davina always factors in an extra twenty minutes' journey time when travelling in London, and the driver, despite the traffic lights and the stink-vibes from the back seat, drives her to her destination with tremendous efficiency. He makes up some of the lost time. Ultimately, the Dame arrives only nine minutes late. She gives him a final ticking off as she climbs out of the car and makes a note to lodge a complaint with his managers before the end of the day.

As she settles herself behind the panellist counter, hot and truly livid, Lord Stevens of Dirkmass and Stirton informs her that a) Sensible Su has just slipped to the toilet and that b) there is no need for her to worry about arriving late as the morning's agenda has anyway been delayed, if not entirely aborted. None of the morning's expert witnesses has yet bothered to turn up.

Dame Davina says: "Well I'm not surprised. It's chaos out there this morning!"

"Worse than usual?" asks Lord Jeremy. He and Su both arrived well over an hour ago. "Su and I were just discussing," he adds, "how we prefer to get ahead of the rush hour by leaving that little bit in advance. One spends less of one's life in traffic jams, and more of one's time actually *getting on with things*. I must say I find it saves a lot of time in the long run."

If she'd had a truncheon handy she might have bludgeoned him to death. Instead, Dame Davina smiles. She says: "Yes. I'm aware of that. I've lived in London for many years, Jeremy. As I say, my driver arrived almost forty minutes late."

"Of course," Lord Jeremy replies.

"And you know what else?" she blurts out. "Not one traffic light - not a single traffic light was functioning between here and Primrose Hill. Can you believe it? *Every single traffic light was out!*"

Lord Jeremy is startled by the news. "Goodness," he says. "That doesn't sound good. They were certainly working when I came in... Well in that case, Davina, I congratulate you on getting here in such good time."

"Thank you, Jeremy," says Dame Davina, partially mollified. "What was so upsetting was the *attitude*... Idiots, everywhere, just *laughing*. My own incompetent driver seemed to think it was funny..."

"Funny?" repeats Lord Jeremy.

"On the pavements, in the cars," she continues, the nightmare replaying in her head... "I can't tell you how silly people were being... How can it be *funny*, all the traffic lights going out? Tell me: how can that be funny?"

Of course, the question is rhetorical. Lord Stevens of Dirkmass and Stirton cannot tell Dame

Davina how that might be funny.

"I suppose it explains the absence of the scientists," he ventures. "… At least, so one hopes… But I begin to fear…" He checks himself. And sticks to the facts. "I understand they're not picking up their phones this morning… Also… so far as one can ascertain, their hotel accommodation, which we kindly supplied on their specific request - not one of them has taken it up. At this point we're not sure if they're even in the city."

Patrick Carfield, Associate Professor of NanoTube Spectroscopy; Diane Addersward, Professor in Microfluidic Biomedical Chemical Engineering; and Nobel prize winning Dr Traupet Maxicon, a roving specialist in Organametalic Metathesis, were all meant to be sharing their findings viz Ozias' fantastical lotion this morning. Last week, in great secrecy and urgency, each had been sent a specimen to analyse. There have been emails between the PAs, confirming receipt etcetera. But no one associated with the Inquiry has communicated directly with any of the experts since.

20

Dame Davina is still so angry about the traffic lights that she's not fully clocked the implications of the situation, and Sensible Su is still on the toilet. But inside Lord Jeremy's healthy, gluten-free gut, there is a growing sense of dread.

Something is happening out there in the world, and this 'Inquiry' doesn't appear to be doing much to prevent it. It's too little, too late. Or too much, too soon? He isn't certain. He can't be sure. He's not a man who tends to listen to his gut, but this....

He slurps on the bottled water and gazes out through the glass wall, onto the empty chair that had yesterday been occupied by Ozias. *Who to put in it now?...* How are they supposed to get to the bottom of all this nonsense if no one can be bothered to turn up to answer the questions?

As previously noted, the Eden Team, responsible for organising Ozias Plume's Mexican retreat, appears to have entirely dropped off the grid. Not one former Eden employee has been willing to answer the Inquiry's questions, not even by email.

Also, the Inquiry has repeatedly reached out to George Houseman. But he's not cooperating either. He sent a written response claiming to know nothing, remember nothing, and politely but adamantly refusing their invitations to come to London and say so in person. He's hunkered down somewhere in Switzerland, according to Ozias, trying to unravel the unholy mess that is – or was – Ozias Plume's evil empire. He's trying (according to Ozias) to return land to Ecuadorian farmers, copper deposits to Congolese miners, chip factories to the pre-pubescent machinists of Bhutan… and so on. It's proving extraordinarily complicated: more complicated, according to Ozias, than it was to build the evil empire in the first place.

In any case, according to Ozias, when George isn't busy at his dismantling work, he is busy cross-country skiing, and cannot be disturbed. It is ridiculous, Lord Jeremy thinks, that this Inquiry can't insist the stupid bastard appears before them. It can't, however (as Lord Jeremy was happy to remind Sensible Su only this morning, before she slipped off to the toilet: *this being an Ad Hoc and Non-Statutory type of Public Inquiry,* he reminded her, *we don't have that privilege.*)

Giggles are infectious. Anyone who was ever once a child knows this perfectly well. Even Lord Jeremy knows this, in his dry fashion. Not that he has ever giggled about anything much. Except once – *years* ago, in his twenties, when Malcolm de Freullily dragged them both into that appalling sex dungeon in Paris, where there were naked everywhere, blatantly having intercourse. The memory flashes through his mind. Unhelpful and irrelevant, and not particularly funny anymore, either. He feels no inclination to giggle. Quite the opposite. Davina's reports regarding the traffic lights this morning are disturbing… The chaos out there is clearly gaining momentum - an exponential acceleration even, or so it appears. Things are falling apart.

A bubble of air makes its way through his healthy colon and releases itself, with some force, into the atmosphere.

Dame Davina pretends not to notice. She examines the witness call sheet laid out on the desk in front of her. If Scientists 1, 2, and 3 can't be located, she's suggesting they don't hang around, but skip directly to the afternoon witness.

Lord Jeremy agrees that this would be a sensible way to proceed.

"Assuming she's bothered to turn up," Dame Davina grumbles, looking over her specs, perusing the Everyday Benches below. "She was here yesterday… Ah! There! Just walking in! Look, Jeremy! Both of them together! I really don't think it's appropriate… I think we should look again at the rules on witnesses being permitted to… For goodness sake they're sitting next to each other. Did they spend the night together? We simply don't know… But *of course* it's going to affect what they tell the Inquiry. It's ridiculous…"

Debs Malone and Ozias Plume are at that moment making their entrance, squeezing into a small space on the Everyday Benches; a small space that wasn't there before, but which appears to have been created out of the goodwill of their neighbours. Ozias is being patted on the back – not by everyone, it should be said: and of course, the

power of celebrity can never be overestimated –
but *the majority* is smiling warmly, gunning for the
Good Guy. It's hardly surprising, thinks Lord
Jeremy. Everyday people tend to be highly
susceptible. They'll believe anything. Follow
anyone. Which is why they need to be protected.

"Do you think our having capitulated to this
Inquiry may have been a dreadful mistake?" Lord
Jeremy asks, thinking aloud. He trusts Dame
Davina. He feels that she is, in this context at least,
very much part of the 'we'. They are batting for the
same team. "I worry it's only lending credibility to
Plume and his abominable stories… You would
have thought, after his performance yesterday,
people might have woken up and realised he was a
madman. They might have seen him for the
fraud *we know him to be*. But looking at the way
they're grinning at him now… One begins to
wonder… Perhaps we should call a halt to all this,
before-"

Dame Davina says: "I think it's a bit late for that.
We should have cracked down on it weeks ago…
And now here we are. We had no choice. There's a
tipping point, isn't there, at which one becomes –
one is *perceived* to be - foolish to ignore
something."

"Is there?" says Lord Jeremy. "I'm not
convinced. I think giving these people oxygen…"

"Plume put out one of his disgraceful little

videos last night, as I'm sure you're aware."

"Of course I am," snapped Lord Jeremy.

"153 million views this morning, last I checked… Do you want to know how many people tuned into the BBC news last night?"

"It's not very relevant."

"109,407."

"So what?" Lord Jeremy sounds very irritable indeed. "Anyone can view a video… Videos mean nothing. It's when the British Government starts responding to them - lending these things credibility by putting on Public Inquiries… Perhaps we should consider whether we're actually doing more harm here than good? If I had my way…" He doesn't finish. If he had his way – what? He would lock Ozias Plume in a faraway dungeon - yes - kick his head in and throw away the key. But would it make any difference at this point?

A silence. Then Dame Davina says: "Last night on the way home, I popped into Marks and Sparks…"

Lord Jeremy leans away from her. "I hope you were careful."

"I didn't need to be," she says. "The place was virtually empty. I've never seen anything like it."

"Cost of living," he says quickly, to sooth himself. "People are feeling the pinch."

"It's more than that."

Another silence.

The truth is, people have stopped buying things. In an unprecedented, unforeseen, unimaginable turn of events, the everydays have gone off shopping. Now, it appears, they're not even interested in browsing.

Lord Jeremy taps his clean fingertips against the long desk, thinks about his end of year dividends, and asks the big question: "Do we have retail spending stats for the weekend yet?"

Dame Davina would have answered - but then Sideline Su returns from the toilet, full of beans and banter. She's holding her phone out in front of her, ready to show them something. "Morning all!" she says brightly. "Or should I say good *afternoon*, Davina!!" Her perkiness is, of course, painful for Dame Davina. Once again, it is fortunate she has no truncheon to hand. "Have you seen this?" asks Sideline Su. "I was on the toilet checking my phone, as you do, and my son Neil- he's at Oxford studying Maths and Computer Science. In his third year. Cruising towards a double first so we're very proud. He's just sent me the most outrageous thing on Insta... It's... nuts. Seriously... *nuts*."

She holds the phone in front of them, touches the screen. Benny Hill music blasts out.

"Oops. Wait. Hang on..." She mutes the sound. "It only happened about fifteen minutes ago, so I don't know how they added the music so quickly."

She touches the screen again… *And action!*…

It is rush hour at Elephant and Castle, South East London, and people have climbed onto the rooves of cars in the middle of a six-lane roundabout. At first glance it looks like just another protest – except – no one's protesting. They're grinning and bowing at one another, and waving each other forward, *after you! No, after* you! They look like courtiers at a Prince Charming ball. Drivers edge round each other or pause to chat. Nobody seems to be bothered, everyone is laughing and smiling - and the traffic is moving.

Sensible Su swallows a chuckle. "The traffic lights are broken!" she says. "Literally, all over London, apparently! Going on-and-off like a mad disco. So people are having to work it out for themselves… Amazing… And there's another video circulating, Neil says. He's trying to get it for me now. Scenes at Palestra House — London's traffic management HQ, as you will know. Neil's going to send it to me… Oops. Wait a bit, here it comes…"

But Lord Jeremy has already whipped out his own device. He's searching Palestra House. Sure enough – *oh my goodness. Oh dear. Oh hell*…

Someone with a camera has got inside the control room. They've done a slo-mo 360 degrees on it, also to Benny Hill music.

It's a very big room. And there's a cartoon brawl

playing out in the middle: a mountain of sprawling bodies. Some, mostly the ones at the bottom of the heap, are looking frantic with rage. Others are simply lying there, holding their stomachs in helpless laughter. Beyond the brawl, in front of a high wall of flashing lights, switches and dials, five or six people appear to be pretending to be concert pianists, prancing around the place, eyes shut tight, waving their arms around *and pressing buttons*.

Sensible Su says, "Yikes." No chuckles to swallow now. "Is it real? So hard to tell these days... It *looks* real..."

Lord Jeremy and Dame Davina are too horrified to speak. They watch the video three times on a loop without saying a word.

And then - some good news at last. A tap on the glass cube door, and an usher, wearing plastic gloves, steps into the room. Professor Diane Addersward is in the building.

"Professor Addersward says to tell you she's here on behalf of all the experts together," says the usher. "But she says she hasn't got long."

"Well that's no good," Dame Davina snaps. "That's clearly not acceptable. We can take her evidence, but she can't speak for anyone else."

Lord Jeremy disagrees. "Beggars can't be choosers," he says miserably. "Let's get her in here before she changes her mind. Let's hear what she's got to say."

21

She states her name and her full address, and it's less complicated than when it was Ozias' turn, because she has an address: a nice, expensive cottage in Oxfordshire. She's driven in this morning, having decided on a whim the previous evening that she couldn't face spending the night in a hotel. She left the expensive cottage forty-five minutes later than she meant to, she says, because she was enjoying her breakfast so much. Her face is very shiny.

The panellists notice this as she explains about the delicious breakfast.

"Amazing skin," says Sensible Su. "Someone's got a good moisturiser!"

Dame Davina and Lord Jeremy have a different response. First, they order a pause to the proceedings.

Then they order organic, fair trade, non-dairy cappuccinos and teas to be sent into the VP cube, with a mountain of fresh, gluten-free cinnamon rolls, and have the speakers that connect the cube to proceedings in the boring room, switched to mute.

"Seems a bit pointless cutting off their sound though," observes Sensible Su. "If they want to know what's being said, they can just ask the people on the Everyday Benches in the break."

"Well, they certainly *could*..." Lord Jeremy

acknowledges.

In any case, now that the media and other vested parties are settled with their ethical beverages and still-warm cinnamon rolls, proceedings can begin once again.

HAZELNUTS

"Of course I examined the lotion," Professor Addersward tells everyone else. "And I discovered numerous ingredients, many of which you may be familiar with." She considers this. "There was nothing very complicated about it. You might have asked an A level student to do the job. Not that I'm complaining." She smiles warmly. "You paid us all very generously, and I thank you for that!"

"If we could stick to the topic," interrupts Dame Davina. "This isn't really an appropriate platform to discuss-"

"Absolutely," agrees Professor Addersward, rolling her eyes at her own silliness, having a good old chuckle. "I do apologise. First, I arrive late. Then I wander off topic… The only question I have…" she pauses. "Actually, it's a question we all had. My lovely colleagues and I, we found it rather funny. We had quite a giggle about it together last night over the Zoom. We were wondering if there'd been a mix up somewhere along the way. Are you certain you sent us all the same samples?"

The panellists don't hesitate to confirm this, though obviously, having played no active part in the process, they haven't the faintest idea.

"… Because we each came up with very different components…"

"HA!" bursts out Ozias from the benches. "Exactly the same here!" he cries. "No matter how many times I sent it for analysis, they came back with different answers."

"Silence!" barks Dame Davina.

"Sorry!" he says. "I'm so sorry... But do tell me, Professor. I can't wait to hear what you discovered in your sample. The last chemist I sent a sample to, swore blind there was nothing in it but hazelnuts. One hundred per cent hazelnuts!"

"One more word from you, Mr Plume, and I will have you escorted from the hearing."

"Sorry," he says again. People around him are beginning to smile. "It's just – It's so crazy! I must have sent it out twenty times. And every result came back different."

Debs, sitting beside him, notices a couple of wagglers moving in. She nudges him. Ozias apologises one more time, mimes zipping his lips, and gestures for the Professor to continue. *After you! No, after you!*

Professor Addersward giggles. And then it becomes clear that she can't stop.

Dame Davina says, "Would you like some water, Professor?"

But it's hopeless. Eventually the wagglers are summoned to escort her away.

Next up, Deborah Malone.

ENGINE MAINTENANCE

Debs' father owns a campervan. Or he did. He died a couple of years ago. Debs' Ma kept the ignition key – somewhere. It took Debs' Ma a while to find it, on a night when Debs was in quite a hurry - but all's well that ends well etc. The campervan works and over the past few months, she and Ozias have become fully engrossed with the rules of good engine-maintenance. It's an old engine by the way. Debs' father was a clever, private man, a car mechanic, serious about engines and disdainful of the new-fangled machines, with all their electronics. Not that it's relevant.

Debs and Ozias have been mostly living in the campervan since that first evening, only really using the hotel on Tottenham Court Road as an address, when required. They've been busy, buzzing around, making the world a better place.

One day, about six weeks ago, over bread and carrot soup, Debs said to Ozias: "It's funny though, isn't it, that all this should be happening in England, of all places. Why us? Why here? Do you suppose it's happening all over the world and we just don't know it yet? I mean," she added, "What's so special about little old England?"

"Hmmm," Ozias replied, tactfully. Then he giggled, because there was nothing to be tactful about. "Well, the Brits – they're not a very happy bunch, these days... Maybe God and/or Ferdinand just got fed up listening to the whingeing..."

Debs and Ozias laughed quite a lot about that.

"But Ozias, the Poms aren't the only ones to whinge," Debs said. "The Yanks whinge. The French whinge. The Germans... Actually - do Germans whinge much? Probably. Your friend Ferdinand's probably been popping up all over the place. I bet he has. Maybe. Or maybe we're the guinea pigs. Who knows?"

"Who knows?" Ozias repeated: it's a question they ask each other a lot. And then: "This soup is delicious."

"Mind blowing," Debs agreed. "If I say so myself. Is there any left or have we finished it?"

AND DISTRIBUTION

At that time, six weeks ago, Ozias was the packaging maestro. He had become a font of quite brilliant packaging ideas, and with the help of Mr Houseman and a mystery team of goblin assistants in far off Switzerland, new types of enticing and practical packaging found its way to the campervan each morning.

It was Debs who thought of the market stalls.

Ozias thought of bars and nightclubs.

Debs thought of the soap dispensers in public lavatories.

It was Barry Deluxe-Kelson, Russell Drisell's one-time brother-in-law, who thought of taking the lotion to the football and the festivals.

That was the masterstroke, truth be told.

And then - who knows what happened? *Who knows?* Debs and Ozias, for all their massive brains, couldn't and cannot, not for the life of them, work it out. But something has been happening: a shift.

One day not very long ago, over broad beans and duck breast (It being summer, they ate it under the stars, beside the campervan, illegally parked, off-road on Hampstead Heath.) Ozias said to Debs: "It feels like we're reaching a tipping point, Debs. It feels like it's got its own momentum now. Do you think it's possible?"

He said it because something beautiful had just occurred. A police car had drawn up beside them: their illegally parked campervan, and their forbidden campfire. The police officer had rolled down his window, looked at the duck breast and the broad beans, and inhaled the scent, long and slow.

"Through the nostrils," the policeman said.

"Long and slow."

Ozias nodded warmly. "The only way," he said.

"It smells good… What did you do with it?"

Debs and Ozias explained at length – something to do with marmalade. The policeman listened solemnly. They offered him some to taste, but he said he was on his way home in any case. He thanked them. And then Debs said: "Don't worry. We won't leave any mess."

And for some reason, that cracked the policeman up. He waved as he drove off, chest shaking, belly wobbling, tears of laughter streaming down his face.

Anyway, Debs thought Ozias might have made a good point. Something was happening. So many people these days were so *nice*.

But how? How was it possible? No matter how hard Debs and Ozias – and Barry - worked to package and dispense, it simply wasn't feasible that their lotion could have reached so many, and so fast.

Ozias agreed: "Logically, it doesn't make sense," he said. "I want to believe it but…"

"*Logically…*" said Debs.

And then they caught each other's eyes, and they started laughing again.

DEBS

Debs Malone was the coolest kid in the school, and the second cleverest after Ozias (who has always been in a freaky league of his own). Ozias Plume, being a late developer, wasn't especially cool until he teamed up with Debs. Together, they were quite a force. Neither seemed to be afraid of much, and they both had very good repartee. From about 14 years old until they both left – Ozias suddenly, aged 16½, Debs, at the normal time - everyone was a little afraid of them. They were the power couple of Park St Alban's Secondary, Reading.

Everyone wanted to impress them. As a consequence, they both grew too big for their boots, and in very different ways, have spent most of their lives paying the price.

The other thing about Debs back then: she was *hot.* By far the hottest girl in Reading. She was a very good actress, too. Everyone assumed she was destined for stardom. But unlike Ozias, Debs did not go to California and become the richest, most Google-searched individual in the universe. Pretty much the opposite. She peaked on the day they offered her a place at RADA. After that – not much. A little bit of acting work here and there. Plenty of odd jobs in between. The rejections made her bitter, and bitterness made her stupid, and stupidity made her lazy (here endeth the lesson).

For a while, Debs' blessings faded away.

But now, here we find her, twenty-seven years after Ozias vanished from her life; three-and-a-half months since he returned. And her face is very shiny.

Age: 43
Nationality: British
Skin: as noted.
Family background: drab.
Financials: drab.
Marital status: single.
Radiance: blinding

She's sitting in the seat recently vacated by the giggling Professor Addersward. Lord Jeremy has taken the precaution of sending strawberries, champagne and quails eggs to the VP Box, and of keeping their speakers on mute. He will send them a brief synopsis of what will have been said in due course.

She's actually rather attractive, Lord Jeremy thinks, looking down at Debs.

Aside from that, he fears the worst.

"Ms Malone," he says, having confirmed her name and address, etc: "First, thank you for coming today. And thank you for being so amenable regarding the time change. As you are aware, the previous witnesses, scheduled for this morning, were variously indisposed. And I want to thank you, on behalf of the panel, for making yourself available at such short notice. Many thanks."

Debs stares at him. She says: "Well I was only sitting a few rows back. It's not much of an inconvenience."

He is shuffling papers: not looking at her.

"…But you're welcome!" she adds, with a smile that lights up her beautiful, shiny face. She has a face like an angel, wide and warm and open, now that the bitterness has gone. "Fire away!"

Lord Jeremy takes a sip from his bottled water. He's scribbling a note on his shuffled papers. Power play. He's taking his time.

Into the void, a confused Sideline Su asks: "Shall I kick us off then?"

Lord Jeremy says: "I-"

But she's already done it. "Shall we begin at the beginning, Miss Malone?"

"Yes absolutely," replies Debs. She thinks about it. "… I'm not quite sure where the beginning is, though."

Behind her, a rumble of laughter from Ozias. And then a ripple of follow up laughter around the room.

Sideline Su frowns. She's not sure either. And she doesn't like being laughed at. She says: "Well I suppose – you met at school, Mr Plume and yourself, is that correct? Were you childhood sweethearts?"

"Actually," Lord Jeremy interrupts, "we might begin at the point where Mr Plume comes to find you at your previous address at Plumtree Court, Emmer Green, Reading. Perhaps you could begin by telling us how many years it was since you had last seen him, what was your relationship until that point, and for what purpose he claimed to be coming to call?"

"Well I *think*," says Debs, "he was coming to see me because he loved me. That is, I know it. And yes, Lady Panellist – to answer your question. We were childhood sweethearts. We were very much in love… and then there was this terrible – very sudden separation. He vanished from my life. I didn't see Ozias again for many years… I only found out why, when he came to find me the other day. But I was very angry with him for a long, long time. You know how it is with relationships… I was going to say *especially when you're young–* But I'm not sure that's true. I think when you fall in love with someone it never dies. Not really. It changes shape, as the years go by – of course - but it's always tremendously powerful. Don't you think so? It never really dies." Debs looks at Lord Jeremy.

She has always been intuitive (and frank and extremely talkative) but she's even more intuitive these days: she's painfully intuitive. She notes his wooden face, and a tensing around the mouth edges. She senses a micro-shrink in his already shrunken heart. She senses his sense of lacking. His sense of failure. A blankness. Lord Jeremy has never been in love. It's something he's read about. Like he's read about ghosts. He doesn't believe in either.

"If you could keep your answers to the point," he says.

Sideline Su thinks he's been a little rude. She likes the way Debs talks. And she too was in love once. She was in love with the man she married: the man who made a fortune in eco-builds in the Nineties and Noughties and who now does everything he can to avoid her. "How *romantic*!" cries Su. "Carry on! What happened when Mr Plume came to find you? Was it a wonderful reunion?"

EMMER GREEN, READING

Debs was shacking up with Russell at that time. (It was their second year together: her longest relationship to date.) He was not an exciting man in any way at all, but she stuck with him because he was kind, and it made economic sense, and at 43 she was weary, for the time being at least, of living her life alone.

She and Russell lived together in a new build

one-bed with home-study, which had been marketed to the young believers of Reading, seven years ago, as part of a highly desirable luxury living development with excellent links to the city. It came almost fully furnished, with the wifi up and running, a built-in smart TV in the bathroom, white pine laminate flooring in the open concept kitchen-diner-lounge, windows that didn't fully open, and hollow, shiny fire doors that may have been made out of plastic. In a million lifetimes, Debs would not have chosen it. And yet, there she was.

Boyfriend Russell owned the flat – rather, he'd put down a 5 per cent deposit on it six-and-a-half years ago, since when the place had lost 17 per cent of its value. Debs contributed to mortgage and living costs, but Russell, who worked for the Council in a job that involved a lot of outward-bound team-building days, paid the greater share, because, he said, as long as Debs was living with him, he didn't want her to feel any unnecessary financial pressure. Also (which he didn't say) because he didn't ever want to feel obliged to add her name to the deeds.

Either way, Flat 16b, Peartree House, Plumtree Court, New Oaktree Lane, Emmer Green, Reading – belonged to Russell and to Russell alone (except of course it didn't, it belonged to the bank.) The New Oaktree Lane development had a gym facility, which Debs and Russell were allowed to use, should they one day feel inclined. As Russell often observed, it was nice to know it was there. Also, every living unit (has this already been mentioned?) came with a built-in smart TV above the bathtub. Unfortunately, Russell's smart TV broke three months after he moved in, due to moisture.

Debs was eating toast when Ozias came to call. She was eating toast with butter, Marmite and marmalade, mixed together, and drinking quite a big tumbler of red wine. It was 9.30pm, so an odd time for him to call, after so long. But Ozias had done his research. He was aware that Russell was on an overnight team building wilderness retreat just outside Maidenhead, and that Deb's shift at the Barley House Studio Theatre bar, which she now managed, ended early on Wednesdays. So when he knocked on the door (having slipped through the building's entrance without alerting her, for fear of being turned away) she'd been home for twenty minutes.

In the moments after she answered his knock, many intense and contradictory vibes whizzed through and between them. Debs thought she might have been dreaming. Because of course, Ozias being as famous as he was, she knew just what he looked like these days. She used to dream of him often. She used to dream of him tipping up at her plastic door and explaining why he'd disappeared. Sometimes, in her dreams, he was carrying the baby, sometimes not. Of course – he couldn't have been carrying the baby. The baby would have been 25 by now. So not exactly a baby anymore. In any case, the baby never was. After Ozias disappeared so suddenly, she got rid of it. She felt, at the time, that she had no other choice, and Ozias never knew anything about it. When he left, she herself hadn't even known that she was pregnant.

So, heavy stuff to carry around, while the acting career flounders, and everything flounders, and the man who ran off and left her becomes the richest and most Google-searched in the world; and when the current substitute is Russell, a kind man, but not exciting, and there's mildew growing inside the built-in TV in the bathroom. Debs carried this stuff around with her a lot. She lugged it here and there, along with the hundreds of failed auditions, and a long list of ways in which the world had done her wrong, and other excuses. She'd not been pregnant again. But Ozias had *eight* children, apparently, and most of them from different women. Sometimes there were photographs of him, cavorting with his children in extravagant places. She used to gaze at those pictures, not hating him anymore- too many years had passed - but definitely feeding her bitterness.

And then there he stood, with his shiny skin. Out of the blue. He looked quite astonished when she came to the door, as if he'd not expected any of his careful research and planning to come to anything. His shiny face lit up.

She was till chewing on the toast.

"Hey," he said. "*Hey*!"

She stared at him. His smile was so wide, and his appearance on her doorstep so unexpected, it took a moment for Debs to comprehend what she was seeing.

Finally, she said: "Ozias, what are you doing?"

"I don't know, Debs! I don't *know*. ... But I've brought you some amazing cream. Lotion. It's a lotion, Debs."

He'd been keeping tabs on her from his side of the world; increasingly, over the years, as his unhappiness expanded. He would slope off to his luxurious study and track her down on something or other – Facebook and Instagram. Lately, he'd used more sophisticated methods. He'd learned, among other things, that she ran a voluntary youth theatre club in Reading. Maybe that was what gave him the idea she might help. Or maybe, the theatre group – and the lotion – were only excuses.

She invited him in.

27

"And did you feel as if no time had passed?" asks Sensible Su, leaning forward in her chair. "It reminds one a teeny bit of *Dr Zhivago*. Was it terribly intense? Did you discuss the reasons for his sudden departure? I mean to say… or did you just leap straight in with the lotion?"

Dame Davina thinks Sensible Su is letting the side down, with her silly and girlish questions. She says: "I'm not sure whether the reasons for Mr Plume's sudden departure from secondary school twenty-six years previously is particularly germane to this Inquiry... and *really*, I do think any comparisons between Dr Zhivago and Ozias Plume…" She smirks. Lord Jeremy smirks too. The VP inmates would have been smirking too, if only their sound had been connected. *"*Ms Malone, when Mr Plume arrived at the flat, what did he tell you about this so-called 'lotion'?"

Debs ignores Dame Davina. Or doesn't hear her. She is fully directing her communications at the only one up there in the box that appears to have a pulse. She says: "Of course we talked about him leaving Reading so suddenly. We talked about it for ages. And really, if only he could've explained it at the time, it might have avoided so much bitterness… I was very bitter, you know."

A little snort from Dame Davina's mic. Hard to tell what's behind it: a mix of irritability, embarrassment - maybe even a large dose her own bitterness. Dame Davina finds it hard to be kind. Despite her late-to-life lesbianism (or perhaps because of it), she finds it especially hard to be kind to attractive women.

"They had to go into hiding… Mr Ustock – that's Ozias' father - had to disappear very suddenly because the police were after him for an armed robbery which he didn't do… Or maybe he did. But he's dead now anyway. Mr Ustock had to do a midnight flit! Ozias didn't even get a chance to pack anything. He wasn't allowed to contact anyone. Nothing. And it was before mobiles… so… They buggered off to Spain overnight. And then Ozias' Dad changed his name from Ustock to – I don't know what he changed it to, actually. Not Plume. Something else. And Ozias had to lie low, or they would have found his dad and carted him off to jail… Anyway..." Debs sighs, smiles, shrugs: *so it goes.* "As I said to Ozias – at least his dad took his boy with him. Because *Mrs* Ustock, as she was called, was a nutcase, bless her. She couldn't have coped alone. Someone had to take care of her, and *Mr* Ustock ... Put it this way. I don't think Ozias would disagree with me. His Dad was fun. He was a live wire. I mean, he was great… but he was a very selfish man."

From his place in the public gallery, Ozias slaps a palm against his forehead. This was meant to be private information. Over the years, he has gone to a lot of trouble, and spent a great deal of money, burying his unrespectable past. But the thing about Debs – then and now – she could never keep her mouth shut. *Never* entrust a secret to Debs Malone. With the best will in the world. You might just as well read out a statement in the House of Commons. Take out a front-page ad in *The Sun*.

Debs falls silent. She turns to Ozias, her shiny face burning.

He shrugs.

She says, still looking at him: "That was meant to be secret… I'm an idiot… I don't know what to say…"

And then he laughs. A big laugh, because he realises quite how little he cares. He says: "Debs! You've already said it! Carry on! Carry on with the story!"

"You say Mr Ustock was a selfish man," Dame Davina slips in: "Were there incidents of inappropriate sexual behaviour?"

"… *What*?" says Debs. "Mr Ustock? A dirty old man?! No!"

Dame Maddy makes a little note. She nods, waves the question aside. "Carry on."

Lord Jeremy is finding Debs very attractive and it's making him livid: livid with Debs, obviously; livid with himself; and above all, livid with Ozias Plume.

Lord Jeremy is imagining Debs and Ozias making love.

Some guys get all the luck.

He's imagining his quinoa and linseed-demented second wife, Emily, currently doing something wasteful like shopping or walking the dog.

Some guys get all the pain.

He's imagining Debs and Ozias making love 27 years ago

Some guys get all the breaks.

He's lost interest in sex, anyway.

Some guys do nothing but complain.

Everything makes him livid. He's imagining Debs, sitting there, nattering away, without any clothes on, and for a moment he forgets to assert his authority.

Sensible Su is saying, "Well, if you don't mind me saying, I think you make a gorgeous couple."

... And then a woman on the Everyday Benches bursts out laughing.

... And someone a few rows behind her stands up. He has a manicured beard and a stylish haircut. He's wearing a tailored overcoat. He is red in the face. And all this laughter is doing his head in. He shouts out: "Can everyone please STOP MUCKING ABOUT!"

This is followed by a beat of surprise, and then laughter from all corners –quite a lot of it.

He looks around him in shock. "This is not a drill, people," he reminds them. "You think it's funny? It's not funny…. Just because you're laughing, *it isn't funny*."

More laughter.

"Stop laughing!"

For a moment it seems the mood in the room may tip into something too joyful to contain. The security wagglers (most of them) are gazing up at the Panellists' Box, awaiting the nod to impose order. They're keen – they're itching – to do it. At least some of them are.

Lord Jeremy, wrenched from his thoughts of a naked Debs, exchanges glances with Dame Davina, and an understanding of the emergency passes between them. They must press on with the questioning as if nothing is happening.

Su misses the memo, needless to say. She's about to voice her disappointment in no uncertain terms - but under the desk, Dame Davina pinches her, hard. And Sensible Su is shocked back to silence. Dame Davina leans into her mic and throws out the most boring question she can come up with.

"Ms Malone," she says, over the laughter, "That evening, when Mr Plume arrived with his 'lotion', unannounced at your address, was he carrying it with him? Could you describe the jar?"

Debs laughs. "The jar? He had a lot more than a

jar with him! He had a whole lorry load of the stuff!"

Flat 16b

First, the catch up. Ozias knew more about Debs' past twenty-six years than she ever would have imagined. It was nice. It was better than nice. It was exhilarating for her, having assumed all this time that he had forgotten her: confirmation that she wasn't insane, as she said to Ozias, during one of the tentative, mini truces that peppered the first couple of hours of their reunion.

It wasn't his fault that her career had never taken off, while his so spectacularly had, and it wasn't his fault he didn't know about the pregnancy. Lots of things weren't his fault. But he did vanish mid relationship, having sworn to love her for eternity. And he did change his name once, and then twice, and then never contact her again. And she was left to deal with the consequences – a broken heart, and an unborn baby. It's not what this story is about. But it should be noted that within the first hours of their reunion, they both laughed and cried a great deal. Ozias' remorse was full-blooded.

During one of the mini truces, Ozias, normally so intuitive these days, said something careless, which was easily misinterpreted. He said: "Am I right in thinking that tonight, Russell is staying on a wilderness retreat outside Maidenhead? He's not coming home, is he?"

Debs bristled at once, evcn after the full-blooded remorse etc. "You're not staying the night," she snapped. "If that's what you're thinking. You can get that idea right out your head. Shitbag."

"I didn't mean it like that," he said. "Actually. Which isn't to say… *obviously*… I meant…" What had he meant? "… Maybe I did mean it like that. I'm sorry. I thought what I meant… what I mean is… is Russell about to appear and do I need to leave? Or maybe what I meant was, is Russell about to appear and wreck this moment for us… Is Russell going to come in and-" Ozias stopped. He was going to say in a humorous way, to lighten the atmosphere, "beat me up?" But he'd seen photographs of Russell. He didn't look like the beating up type. To put it mildly. He looked like a perfect citizen. A little soft. A little fearful. A waggler *extraordinaire*. So it would have been facetious. Disingenuous. Potentially unkind. Ozias knew Debs. He'd known her for years. And he was mostly very intuitive these days. Plus, it hardly took an empath to understand that Russell and Debs were not a match made in heaven.

Luckily – for both Ozias and Debs, as it transpired – she'd just poured herself a third and Ozias a second glass of wine. So – it would have been weird if she'd chucked him out, despite having called him a shitbag.

Anyway, when she said "shitbag", Ozias felt a tremendous pang. The years had melted away, back to the days when people dared to call him things like shitbag: the days when he and Debs did the things that people do, when they are young and passionately in love - call each other shitbag – *yes!* Fuck a lot, make each other laugh, discuss the meaning of the universe...

He giggled. With his shiny face. He was so happy to see her.

At that point Debs' face wasn't shiny. But the sound of his laughter made her laugh too; against her will.

He said: *You cannot begin to imagine how much I have missed you.*

She said (bristling again): *Well you had a funny way of showing it. For twenty-six years or whatever.* She felt bitter again; and angry with herself for having let him into the flat. "What do you want, anyway? Why are you here?"

So he explained. That night in Mexico, he said, after he left Jacinda and Chak in the banana leaf dining room, as he trundled off to find George Houseman in his hammock to discuss the urgent dismantling of his empire, it had hit him-

"Like a thunderbolt, Debs. I realised how mad it was! All these years, I've been tracking you ... never making contact but always knowing where you were, who you were with…"

"Creepy," Debs observed.

He laughed. "I know! Debs, I know!"

"Why didn't you just come and find me?"

"Too scared," he said. "I think that's what it was. Or too proud. Or too ashamed. Or too stupid. I thought you hated me."

Debs shrugged. "You thought correctly."

"I realised there'd never been – there had *never* been a time when I didn't wonder where you were, how you were doing…"

"I was doing *very badly* most of the time," she said. And for a moment she felt quite overcome with self-pity, and anger – and (of course) relief that she wasn't insane or insignificant etc: that she had meant as much to him - and so on…

It was hard for her to separate his abandonment, her failure, and his worldly success. She wondered aloud – as was her wont - whether her strength of feeling at seeing him again was exacerbated by his dazzling fame – because here they were in the luxury living unit with the broken TV that belonged to Russell; and here was Ozias, the most Google-searched man on earth, and possibly one of the richest.

"Not the richest anymore!" he told her, triumphantly. "I've been giving it all away! Or I'm trying to. It's proving very complicated. Debs, you have to let me tell you about the lotion!"

29

Rewind. Quickly. To the Mexican Retreat.

Jacinda and Ozias didn't see each other again until breakfast. Ozias hadn't been keen to share a bed with her, knowing – or as good as knowing – that she and Chak had so recently been rolling around in it together. He didn't want Chak vibes in his own bed. Any more than he much wanted Jacinda vibes, come to that. In any case – he didn't want to go to bed. He wanted to explore, and find the turtles, and listen to jungle noises. Also, he wanted to strategise. There was so much to do. So much to celebrate... And everything was suddenly so *funny*.

At breakfast, Ozias tried again. He told Chak and Jacinda, who were enjoying themselves putting on a show of hiding the erotic charge between them, that if they wanted shiny skin and to feel at one with nature, also, to find lots of new things funny-

Chak guffawed. "I find enough things funny already, thank you so much chum!"

Jacinda said: "I adore nature."

… they should do what he and George had done and apply a little of the mystery lotion to a part of their body that felt uncomfortable.

Chak and Jacinda both very much demurred. They said: *seriously Ozzie. We're worried. We think you've gone nuts.*

But they can't have been that worried, apparently, because later the same morning they returned to civilisation – or to California – sharing the same chopper, leaving Ozias, the lotion, and George Houseman alone at the retreat.

30

Team Eden and the Mexican house servants were located in a hidden encampment, just around the bay: within quick and easy reach of Ozias' banana leaf retreat, should he want something, but out of his sight and hearing.

What Ozias wanted, that morning, was to go to the encampment with his lotion and his new best friend, George Houseman, so they could test it out on some willing volunteers. What Ozias wanted was willing volunteers.

The encampment consisted of thirty or more yurts and tipis, very luxurious, arranged in a large circle, with a clearing in the middle. A generator provided power for all the usual American home comforts. The Team Edenites, being young professionals, complained to one another incessantly about their appalling jungle working conditions, but the conditions were far from appalling, and the Mexican faction, less spoilt for the most part, tended to laugh at the Californians behind their backs.

Ozias stood in the centre of the clearing. He placed the dirty pot of lotion at his feet and called everyone to lay aside whatever they were doing and to gather round. Houseman, beside him, wearing bathers borrowed from Ozias and the yellow Airtex t-shirt he'd arrived in, cupped his hands to his mouth and repeated, between bouts of blissful laughter:

"Hot off the press!"

Ozias beamed, because Houseman was smiling. He said: "Why are you saying that?"

Houseman replied: "Good News. Hot off the press."

They found this very funny.

Slowly, reluctantly, the 'volunteers' emerged from their luxurious tents. They formed a tentative circle around the two giggling men and waited to be told what was going on.

"Guys!" Ozias cried, when it seemed that enough people were present, and he and George had finally stopped laughing. "Has anyone got an ache or a pain?… Anything at all?"

Obviously, no one replied.

"Serious question, guys," Ozias said. "Literally, anything... You don't even have to say what it is. Just… literally .. any problem you have, all you need to do is step a little bit closer to *this jar*." He pointed at the jar with both hands and glanced at Houseman. They were aware, suddenly, of how absurd this must have sounded. They started laughing again.

Houseman was the first to recover. Wiping his eyes, he said: "It may not work, by the way. This is a very new theory, and actually Ozias, you tried it on Jacinda and Chak, didn't you, and they were completely immune. So. In which case…" He shrugged. "Even so, it's worth a try."

Ozias nodded: "Perhaps Jacinda and Chak didn't have anything wrong with them," he said. "That's what I'm thinking. They were 100 per cent in good shape, so they didn't need any lotion." This makes him laugh again. But then it makes him sigh. He stops laughing. He says: "You can't win 'em all, can you Mr Houseman? You cannot win 'em all."

The general assumption among employees was that George and Ozias were high. This was quite amusing for them and would be excellent fodder for mockery and dissection later in the day, but as things stood it was - if not terrifying, then something pretty close. Ozias frightened everyone at the best of times because he was hard to read, hard to please and notoriously quick to fire people. And although Houseman looked, on first glance, to be quite a boring man, he was nevertheless an unknown ingredient, and his uninhibited laughter and weird affinity with Ozias was extremely disconcerting.

Ozias' question remained unanswered. Not one

of them moved or spoke.

"Seriously. This is-"

Ozias paused. Being suddenly quite intuitive, he sensed the intense discomfort around him and was moved to apologise. Which he did very nicely, with Houseman listening and nodding solemnly beside him. When Ozias had finished apologising, Houseman said, sincerely:

"Yes, I'm sorry too."

There was a moment when it seemed the two of them might once again melt into laughter, but they didn't.

A pause.

And a longer pause.

Lots of jungle noises, and the lapping of distant waves.

And then a yelp from a youngish man named Timmie, who had a master's degree from Harvard in renewable agri-tech touristry and wellness. He was clutching at his stomach.

"Ah-ha!" cried Ozias joyfully. "Are you in pain?!"

"My stomach!" Timmie wailed. He doubled up and fell to his knees.

Beside him, colleague Carrie, 35 years old and always offended about something, stepped forward to voice her offence about this: whatever this was. She was going to say something. She was going to express her dismay/lodge a complaint/lead a revolt.

But then – a spasm in the descending colon! A serious and incapacitating explosion of pain, the like of which she would never have imagined possible.

She cried out, "Oh my p-p-p-ooper!", and fainted.

"Ha!" cried Houseman. "Another one down! Quick, quick, Plume. Where's the pot? Pass the jar! *Hurry*!"

One by one, down they went, their screams of pain interrupting everything they had to say except – conveniently or mysteriously - the name of whichever part of their anatomy to have been struck. It all happened very quickly. A couple of the Mexicans ran off, but ultimately the Californians were more afraid of the jungle, and of going out on a limb, so they took the punishment: stood in frozen fear until their turn came to cry out, and collapse to the floor.

Ozias and George had not thought things through very thoroughly. Perhaps they had not been expecting their theories to have been proved quite so bang on. In any case – while the employees lay in the mud, writhing and screaming in pain, Ozias and George had to come to a decision about the medication. Could they simply administer it, without people's consent? It didn't seem right. On the other hand, the lotion would surely put them all out of their misery.

"We have to ask them," Ozias said. "We have to say to them – do they want the pain to go away? Do they want shiny skin? Do they want to find everything serious but also funny?… Or do they want to… stay as they are?"

A pause. Ozias and George looked around them at the circle of writhing bodies.

"What do you reckon?" Ozias asked. He could feel his lips twitching. "Shall we ask them?"

George said yes. He took a lung-full of air, cupped his hands to his mouth once again, and yelled over the groaning: "Attention, everyone! Attention please! We can see you are all in a lot of discomfort. *If you would like us to offer you some lotion to take the pain away, please raise your hand…"*

But people were too preoccupied with their discomfort to do anything like that, and the groaning made it harder for them to hear.

Houseman tried again. He was in danger of giggling. Not because he didn't sympathise with their pain. On the contrary. He felt for them deeply. On the other hand, the situation was also very funny.

Ozias, being intuitive, noticed his friend was on the cusp of losing control. He cleared his throat. Very slowly and very clearly, he said:

"Guys! Listen up! George and I are going to go round the <u>circle</u>, and we're going to offer <u>each of</u>

you some _lotion_ to make you feel _better_. We don't know what the long-term effects may be, or even the medium term effects, but so far Mr Houseman and I can 100 per cent confirm that the short term effects are – very jolly. If you would _like_ the lotion, say _YES_. If you would _NOT_ like the lotion, please say _NO_. Ok?"

No one replied at that point, either. But when it came to it, and the two men were crouched solicitously over each person, asking if they would like to be cured, they all said:

YES.

Multiple lawsuits loomed.

But only if the lotion didn't work, and happily it did.

DEBS

Dame Davina says: "A whole _lorry load_ of jars?"

She snorts, to denote her disbelief.

"You're telling me [she continues] that Mr Plume arrived at your door at 9.30pm in the evening, unannounced, having snuck through the main entrance of the building, we're not certain how, and that there he stood, a man you'd not spoken to for almost thirty years, carrying 'a whole bunch of jars', _and you let him in?_"

Debs gazes at Dame Davina, who is too fat to be healthy, much too fat; and whose swollen form seems to Debs (always intuitive, nowadays exceptionally so) to be radiating anger, physical discomfort and self-loathing. Debs feels sad for her. She feels, for a moment, the stultifying weight of Dame Davina's lack of joy. She says: "I'm really sorry…" and realises there's no helpful way to finish the sentence. She starts again. "I did let Ozias in. Of course. But I'm not sure why him arriving with lots of jars as opposed to just one jar is the part you're finding hard to believe? Also, actually, he didn't *arrive* with lots of jars. They appeared a bit later. What happened was – well, everything arrived together. Russell appeared out of nowhere… I think you've got Russell coming to give evidence tomorrow morning, is that right?"

"Traffic-lights allowing!" smiles Sideline Su. A little joke. "But, yes. You are correct. He's due in at noon tomorrow, I believe."

"Please. Continue," Dame Davina says.

"Russell arrived at about – it must have been a short time after midnight, I think. By then lots of things had already happened. Ozias was still there, obviously. He'd already brought out the lotion: literally, just plopped it on the carpet between us, and I won't go into the details, but my experience was very similar to Ozias', George's, Team Eden's etcetera. I don't know if you're familiar with the chakras, *but oh my goodness*, my sacral chakra!" Debs pauses, rolls her eyes– "… I cannot describe to you the pain… Anyway, it didn't last for long. The point is, by the time Russell arrived, I had already applied the lotion. I had already - joined the Brady bunch as it were. It was all over, if you know what I mean?"

Dame Davina looks so very sour; Debs doesn't wait to be reassured. She continues:

"Russell was meant to have been staying the night at the wilderness outward bound thing, as you know - but he got a bit homesick, so he'd told his supervisor he was having an allergy attack and asked to be excused."

Lord Jeremy wants to know whether Russell was angry to see Ozias in his flat when he got home. It's not very relevant to the Public Inquiry, but he really wants to know. So he asks the question in sardonic manner to demonstrate to Debs that he doesn't actually care.

Debs says: "He was *extremely* - disconcerted, yes. Ozias was a very famous, very controversial figure. People hated him for all sorts of reasons…"

"Unfortunately," says Sideline Su, sounding perky but also regretful, "I think many people still do."

"- So, it was obviously a bit weird for him to see Ozias standing there with me … Plus I'd never really mentioned to Russell that Ozias and I used to know each other."

"Why ever not?" (From Lord Jeremy, leaning

into the mic.)

Debs shrugs. "It never really came up."

32

There was time, between Deb's chakra realignment
and the unwelcome arrival of Russell, for the two
old flames to cover plenty of ground. The past was
the past. They had nothing more to say on that.
More compelling by far, was *everything else*: their
shiny faces, their shiny outlooks. The bounciness of
everything, everywhere. The funniness of being
reunited again, and all the time they wasted,
pretending to have forgotten each other.

"Shall we get a dog?" Ozias said.

Debs thought he was jumping the gun, though
only in a chronological sense. Of course they
should have a dog. (Also, most definitely, if they
were lucky enough, a family!) But for the moment
they lived in different countries, were romantically
attached to different people. Who would look after
the dog, for example, when they were both busy
elsewhere? Also – clearly, their partners might have
something to say about it. They would need to be
informed.

This was jumbled thinking.

Their partners needed to be informed of quite a
lot of things, now that it was obvious the two were
back together, joined for the rest of their earthly

lives, never to be separated again. In the meantime, Ozias' magical lotion raised burning questions: more burning, even, than their desire to fuck each other, which was vast.

Debs thought it would be disrespectful to consummate their reunion here at the Luxury Living Unit, with the deeds being in Russell's name, and the living unit being his pride and joy.

This was boring of Debs, Ozias thought (and said). On the other hand – on the other hand… They'd waited this long.

He sighed.

The sigh was so heartfelt it made Debs laugh until there were tears rolling down her cheeks, and her stomach ached.

She said: "Where did you find this magic potion? What is it? How long does it last?"

"It seems to last forever," he said. "So far as I can tell… As for what it is and where I got it…"

He told her more or less the same story he would tell to the Ad Hoc Non Statutory Public Inquiry three months hence, but he told her in more detail, because she asked better questions, and didn't interrupt to nit-pick. He described to her the effect the magic lotion seemed to have on almost everyone who used it, and that so far – of course it was still early days – the effects only seemed to get better, softer, and more integrated, with the passing of time. She wanted to know how many people had used it, to his knowledge. He told her about Team Eden and George Houseman, Jacinda and Chak. He said his mind kept returning to the puzzling immunity of Jacinda and Chak. Back in Los Angeles, he'd offered the lotion to his entire house staff, which was quite large, and most of them had accepted it. Jacinda had been livid, because it had taken its toll- not so much on the quality of their work, but on the style.

"Just as efficient, but more carefree... They're always laughing. And then, there's no question of anyone pretending the 'master/servant' situation isn't weird and absurd. So - It made Jacinda feel jumpy... but I don't want to be disagreeable about Jacinda," Ozias adds. "You'll probably meet her anyway... And by the way, I'm not blaming Jacinda...We are the way we are... The point is – Debs, I've been trying so hard to track down not just Ferdinand - Octavius – I mean the guy on the beach – I've been trying to discover the ingredients in his mystery lotion."

The mystery man and his magic potion, Debs said, giggling haphazardly.

Mystery lotion,
Magic potion,
Blind devotion
Fatuous notion.
Ha ha
Public emotion. Coastal erosion. *Massive*

explosion. Do the locomotion.

It held them up for a bit.

"I've sent out search parties. We spent three nights in the jungle –George and me, roaming around, dodging snakes and so on, *totally unafraid* Debs, that's the thing. Seriously – think of something that frightens you – I mean. Something that used to frighten you. Or whatever. Death. Take death. Are you afraid of death?"

It occurred to Debs that this wasn't something she was terribly frightened of. She said: "Think of something else."

He thought of various things… "Prison? Vampires? Ghosts? Bankruptcy? Intense physical pain? Being buried alive? Having your eyes pecked out by vultures?"

A pause, while she considered these options: and considered them fully: *felt* them even.

She said: "Hmmm."

He nodded. "See what I'm saying?"

She wasn't sure that she did.

He said: "It doesn't matter. It's just something I've noticed. It's something in the lotion. Very liberating."

"Anyway, the thing I've learned – one of the things I've learned - Ferdinand only appears when he wants to. He appeared in LA the other day. I was in a traffic jam. The passenger door opened which wouldn't have been possible, because you always lock the passenger door in downtown LA for obvious reasons, and then there he was, in the passenger seat... By the way he's not called Ferdinand. He changes his name. He changes everything... I've only met him twice. I think. Or five or six times actually– if you count in my dreams... He's called Jupiter in my dreams, which I suppose is a cross between Juniper and my own subconscious feelings regarding his magical power-"

Debs didn't much care about what his name was, in the LA traffic jam or in Ozias' subconscious. Her own mind was spinning with far bigger possibilities.

"The point is, Debs," he said–

They were sitting on the floor, like a pair of teenagers, both leaning in, talking more intensely than either had spoken about anything since – he left her behind in Reading, 26 or so years ago. "The point *is* Debs, I can't control any of it! Nothing. Ferdinand appears when he wants to appear. And whatever it is he puts in the jars – We've sent it for analysis to seven different labs so far, and every time they've come back with a different answer.

"The point *is*," Debs said, "I've not felt like this since – I honestly haven't felt like this since I was born, probably. I feel..."

"Very springy," nodded Ozias. "It's beautiful, isn't it?"

"Beautiful!" she sighed. And then, bolt upright, suddenly: "Ozias, you realise, don't you, it might be the answer to everything!"

"YES!!" Ozias cried. He nodded wildly. *That's just what I've been thinking!"*

She grinned.

He grinned.

They nodded and grinned.

"We could–" But she was interrupted - not by Russell, not yet, but by a flash of sudden movement at the window, and a thunderous crash. It was the sound of a heavy load being dropped from a great height. They both heard it. Rather, they couldn't have missed it. The entire, shoddy building shook. Deb's cheap wine bottle rattled on Russell's ugly coffee table. The lamps wobbled. A picture slid off the wall. The sound was easily startling enough for Debs to forget what she was saying. She and Ozias stared at each other.

In unison, they moved to the window. One of the key selling points to the New Oaktree Lane Luxury Living Development was its emphasis on above-and-beyond resident safety and security. This involved the display of posters encouraging use of handrails on communal stairways, CCTV cameras on every corner, windows that wouldn't open, and 24-hour lighting on all the tarmac outside. At New Oaktree Lane, darkness never descended. In one way. In another way, of course, it never lifted.

Anyway. So Ozias and Debs moved to the window, and (since it didn't open) pressed their noses against the glass.

There was a lorry out there - or a juggernaut, more like. It appeared to be shuddering and bouncing, as if from its impact with the ground.

"*How the hell?*" muttered Debs. "Was that-? Did that -? Did you see that? How did it happen?… Did you see it dropping? It dropped! It just dropped from the sky!" She giggled. "Management'll go tonto… Not even bicycles are allowed on this bit of the tarmac–"

Ozias said: "It's *bouncing.*"

"Are we dreaming?*"*

*"*I think we should get down and investigate. Quickly. Before someone calls the police."

Debs said: "… It's *still bouncing.*"

It was clearly still bouncing.

Debs didn't want to waste time looking for her house keys. She and Ozias left a shoe in the door to keep it from closing and scampered down the stairway together. Together they burst out of the building.

Towering before them, shuddering and growling, there bounced an almighty lorry. Its lights were on, its engine was running, its door hung open - but the cabin was empty. It shuddered and bounced, apparently abandoned.

And then along came Russell.

Daisy Waugh

DAY THREE

Russell is nervous. His story isn't hanging straight, and he's more than a little star struck by his role in these nationally significant - globally significant - proceedings. He fidgets. He talks too much. His body language is servile.

It brings out the bullying instincts, never far from the surface, in our two least appealing panellists. Lord Jeremy, especially, enjoys contrasting the smartness of his own persona with the efforts of less worldly men. In any case, for a man like Lord Jeremy, tall and slim and good at cricket, Russell Drisell is easy meat. And even though Russell's evidence is meant to undermine the preposterous Plume/Malone narrative, thereby helping to maintain Lord Jeremy's beloved status quo, still Lord Jeremy can't resist making things disagreeable for him. So here he is: he's leaning into his microphone.

"I'm confused, Mr Drisell. Are you saying someone hacked into your account?"

Russell Drisell has not come here expecting to answer difficult questions. The way they put it when they invited him in, he had understood he would be treated gently. He feels a bit sick.

"Do you mean my Instagram account?" he says.

"By my reckoning…" Lord Jeremy leans back, glances at Dame Davina, "By *our* reckoning," he amends (Sideline Su's reckoning is neither here nor there.) "The image of you standing beside Mr Ozias Plume would have been posted within an hour or so of your first encountering him and his 'magical lorry' outside your flat at New Oaktree Lane."

"… Are you talking about my Instagram?" Russell Drisell says again, mind scrambling. He feels very sick, and now there is armpit sweat to contend with, too. He's fully showered this morning and his clothes are nice and clean, but he worries that people might smell something. "I hardly ever use Instagram myself as I consider it a waste of my time. Also, having myself seen the lorry, I do not agree with you that it was in any way a 'magic lorry'. The Science is clear on this… Yes, there was a lorry. However, there was certainly nothing 'magic' about it."

"Thank you Mr Drisell. We appreciate the clarification," Dame Davina says. "I think Lord Stevens was being ironic when he referred to it as 'magical'."

Russell Drisell nods: "Oh, good."

"But to return to the Instagram," Lord Jeremy continues, "I think you used your Instagram that evening, no? The evening you met Ozias Plume for the first time."

"Negative," Russell says. "I don't recall doing that at all..."

"But the post is *there*, for all to see!" chuckles

Lord Jeremy.

Russell furrows his brow as if perplexed. "I suggest my account may have been hacked."

Lord Jeremy shakes his head. "But we can see *your responses to the comments* below the post!"

"I don't recall any comments or any responses. As I say, I dislike Instagram. I hardly ever use it."

"In response to jamieturner9083, you wrote: 'He's actually really down to earth, really normal and natural. A super guy.' … In response to liam_mac32: 'We had a very interesting chat.' In response to lulugrrlpower14: 'He's smaller than he looks in pictures!' … There are several other exchanges. I could go on. It was – is – your most popular post by some way."

Russell Drisell is picking at the skin between his fingers. He, too, is leaning into his microphone, but his posture is more of a hunch. It's because he's trying to manoeuvre himself out of a situation: a lie that he hasn't thought through, and which no one believes, and which – even though he knows he isn't actually 'a liar' - is making him seem like 'a liar', due to the fact that in this instance he happens to have told a mistruth.

The Ad Hoc Non Statutory Public Inquiry has looked him up on Instagram– not a difficult feat. The post, and beneath it, the message from Russell's former brother-in-law, Barry DeLuxe-

Kelson, is, indeed, there for the world to see!

Russell has come here to offer his version of the evidence, because he, like Lord Jeremy, believes in the status quo. Any status quo. He doesn't particularly want to land Barry DeLuxe-Kelson in trouble. He certainly doesn't want to upset an important man like Sir Nicholas James. He just wants everything to be normal again, and for that to happen, Debs' and Ozias' story about bouncing lorries and magic potions has to be debunked. The lorry didn't bounce, no matter what the CCTV cameras show. It's fake footage. He never saw it bouncing.

Right now he's telling blatant mistruths about the Instagram, and he's not even thought to cover his tracks. How can he have imagined no one would check?

Russell is not a bad man. Far from it. He has a soft heart. He is gentle. He is capable of extraordinary kindness. But the newspaper headlines these past few weeks: the empty streets, the laughing people, the traffic light situation yesterday, and then the scene this morning at the bus stop – they've combined to upset him greatly. *He just wants everything to be normal again.*

In the big boring room, a painful silence lands. Lord Jeremy enjoys it because, though this is not something he would dream of listing under 'interests and hobbies', he can't help having a nice time when he's publicly confirming his place in the hierarchy of men.

And Russell is squirming.

From the Everyday Benches, Debs Malone and Ozias Plume long to rescue him. Debs was never in love with Russell Drisell, but she feels his fear and humiliation in the moment and it's difficult for her not rush up to him as he sits there, sweating and picking at his skin. She wants to throw her arms around him, distract him, make him laugh, tell him to sit straight and stop being a pussy… *There's nothing to be scared of,* she wants to say.

Ozias was never in love with Russell Drisell either. On the other hand, of course, he loves him now. And he loves Debs. And he feels her anguish, and he feels Russell's anguish. He toys with the idea of saying *he* hacked the Instagram account, just to get Russell off the hook.

But then Russell breaks the deadlock. He says:

"Ohhhh, you mean *that* post! I do apologise. I was confused. I thought you were referring to something else." He laughs. "Silly me!" Softly, he swipes at his sweaty forehead. "I'll forget my own head one of these days!"

Lord Jeremy leans back and says, "Indeed."

And then Dame Davina says: "Tell us something about the moments *leading up* to the photograph, Mr Drisell."

Russell hesitates.

"You arrived home from the wilderness adventure in Maidenhead," Lord Jeremy prompts him, "because you were feeling a little bit homesick... And what did you find there? Did you, for example," Lord Jeremy offers a wry smile, "as Miss Malone and Mr Plume both contend, find a bouncing lorry?"

Sensible Su pulls a rueful sort of a face. She adds: "We also have the CCTV footage of course…"

Dame Davina doesn't bother to look at Sensible Su. She looks out at the boring room and says, coldly: "The CCTV footage to which Ms Lee refers, as we know, only surfaced on social media a few weeks ago, long after the event, and is certainly a fake. Security Management Services, which provides security for the Oaktree development, has not - and will not - verify it. Thank you, Ms Lee, for the opportunity to clarify that point. Mr Drisell, please continue. You returned from the wilderness adventure at about 12.30am, is that correct?"

Russell Drisell brightens. His shoulders lift. His eyebrows lift. At last, they can stop talking about the Instagram! He says, "Yes, that is correct. I arrived back at Oaktree about 12.30am. Everything was quiet and normal, and I remember I was looking forward to getting home, having a nice glass of something. A hot bath. And catching up with Debs, of course." He pauses, remembering his relationship with Debs, and how it is now defunct. Looking back, it is amazing to Russell that they were ever in a relationship at all. Debs was gorgeous – of course. Well out of his league! But he can see now – in fact he is constantly reminding himself - how little they ever really had in common. And honestly, the way she's been since Ozias Plume turned up, Russell doesn't recognise her. Giddy and silly. And irresponsible and hateful. And dangerous. She is an embarrassment to everyone: him, his family, the Oaktree development, the people of Reading. He can't imagine how he was foolish enough to have cared for her. *Perhaps*, he thinks, *he never really did?*

He did, though. She has broken what was ever left of his fragile heart.

In any case, as he sits there, preparing to dish the dirt, he feels an undertow – quite a powerful undertow. It turns out he hates to do this to her. He sent her an email a few weeks back, attempting to say as much. He was angry with her back then. Now, with the way things are going, there's more at stake than his wounded pride, his broken heart – his visceral loathing of Ozias Plume.

Civilisation is on the brink. *CIVILISATION IS ON THE BRINK!*

Dearest Debs, [he wrote], *I do not want to wake up*

one morning and find that I've been on the wrong side of history.

You used to be a good person who shared my values. Today I cannot recognise the person who I thought might one day be my partner-for-life. This is why I have decided to speak up, on behalf of myself and others in the community at large with my shared values. I have been invited to talk at the urgent Public Inquiry and I have agreed to share my truth related to the current crisis the nation is in. This is for the reasons stated above. I am regretful that what I say will not reflect well on you or on your new 'partner', Mr O. Plume.

He signed off, *I wish you all the luck in world.* But it was not the case.

Debs made quite a few attempts to interact with him before and after she received the email – in person and via the usual electronic pathways.

Russell rebuffed them all.

34

And now here he is, in this significant room, rubbing his hands on his thighs. He had been looking forward to this moment, if only to redeem himself to himself: but now he's not so sure. He's confused. What has he come here to say? He's rehearsed it so often, and now he can't remember.

He has come to defend himself – and also, of course, civilisation...

He has come to say that the lorry wasn't bouncing.

The lorry wasn't bouncing.

And yes, he attempted to call the authorities.

The authorities weren't answering the phone–

I miss you, Debs.

He has come to say– Be Kind. Stay Safe. Not all disabilities are visible. The lorry wasn't bouncing–

I miss you, Debs.

Hold the handrail - Mind the gap - Follow the Science –Share the values - STOP THE LAUGHING.

The lorry wasn't bouncing. It was not bouncing.

Debs, I'm sick and I think I'm dying.

He's wishing he was anywhere else. Above all he is trying not to think about Debs and Ozias, sitting behind him, laughing about everything in the whole wide world, including him.

Perhaps they're right to laugh? Maybe it is funny? Maybe everything is funny, including him, and civilisation being on the brink, and the fact that he is dying?

Is it funny that he's dying?

Well, of course it is, in a way.

A millisecond of comfort quickly dismissed. Russell shakes his head. Flicks it away.

This has been a big couple of months for Russell Drisell. He's been shitting blood. And he's been Googling what that might mean. It started shortly after Debs waltzed off into the sunset with the most famous man in the universe.

Russell has thought about his own death more often and more intensely in the last two months than in the rest of his life put together.

Debs whispers to Ozias: "He's lost a lot of weight. Do you think he's all right?"

Ozias doesn't think he is all right.

It's not the point.

Here sits Russell. Sweating into his clean clothes, preparing to tell his mistruths. He tells himself he's ready to start talking. Debs needs to be stopped. The laughter has to stop. Everything has to *stop.* The lorry wasn't bouncing. He just wants everything to be normal again.

BABBLING

"I found Debs talking with a familiar looking person – I unfortunately didn't recognise him at first, because what would Ozias Plume be doing on New Oak Tree Lane in the middle of the night? And why in the world would such a person be chatting with my then girlfriend?"

A pause. Some scatterings of laughter quickly muffled.

Russell looks ineffably sad.

"… The lorry," he says clearly, "was not bouncing."

"But there was a lorry?" says Sensible Su.

"Oh yes."

Another pause.

"…And?" Dame Davina is growing impatient. "If you could speed up a bit, Mr Drisell. We have a lot to get through."

"Well… of course, when I saw the lorry, I wanted to call security. You may not be aware, but vehicles are not permitted onto that area of the Oaktree Estate. We aren't even permitted to put our cycles there. For safety reasons…

"I discovered Debs and Ozias Plume, both in a state of high excitement. Jabbering, I would call it. They said the lorry had 'bounced out of the sky', or some such nonsense. And they were trying to open the back of the lorry to see what was inside. And they were giggling in a way that definitely suggested to me that they had been drinking, and they were babbling about a so-called 'magic potion'."

"What did you think about that?" asks Sideline Su, who feels she hasn't said much for a while.

"I thought they had obviously consumed a few too many alcoholic beverages. However, I was keen to maintain a pleasant attitude at that point."

"But you went ahead and called Security, did

you?" (Sideline Su)

"That is correct," replies Russell. "I called Security. Very much so. I called Security, as I am sure your records show. However, there was no reply. Unfortunately, Oaktree's 24-hour Security switches to an automatic answering facility after 9pm. Callers are advised to contact the police in an emergency…"

A pause. Russell looks uncomfortable. Dame Davina says: "And yet you never called the police. Perhaps you didn't think this was an emergency?"

Russell shakes his head. "I did feel this was an emergency: very much so. I was about to call the police. However, I was prevented from doing so by *Plume.* He had jumped up into the driving seat and he was dragging Ms Malone to sit beside him. Next thing I knew he had placed the vehicle into gear and had commenced to edge the vehicle in a forward direction."

"But you didn't call the police?" persists Dame Davina.

"Ozias Plume didn't want the police called. He kept saying, *no.* "

"Was he threatening you in any way?" (Lord Jeremy asks hopefully.)

Russell doesn't appear to hear him. "At that point I had already commenced to dial emergency services, as all the alarm bells were going–" He counts them off on his fingers. "We had drunk driving, wc had potentially a narcotics situation. Also, potentially, a mental health-type situation: I could already see that Plume had a very strong mental hold on Debs. Ms Malone."

Debs tuts. She rolls her eyes. But she doesn't interrupt.

"At that moment she was almost like a different person. This was the moment when it started coming clear to me, how I didn't really know Ms Malone at all," he says. He's gathering momentum now, growing in confidence, beginning to enjoy the spotlight, and the sound of his story. "It was a highly precarious situation. Whatever way you looked at it. They were acting illegally, as I continued to point out to them. And in spite of this they *would – not - stop LAUGHING*."

Splutters of laughter from every corner of the room. More laughter than half an hour ago: much more laughter than yesterday, and fewer attempts to muffle it. The panellists note this – even Sideline Su notes it. Su doesn't say anything because she wants to know what happened next. Lord Jeremy and Dame Davina's non interruption is more strategic. Their minds are whirring. They are breathing through their nostrils, trying to keep the dread at bay. They are on full alert, noting the hum of the crowd, calculating how best to defuse it. They wait for Russell to continue.

"… And Debs," Russell says at last, "… *Debs* …

I wanted Debs to come back with me in the flat and not get involved. But she wouldn't listen. She grabbed my phone out of my hands. And off they drove."

"They drove off with your phone?" Sensible Su is rightly confused.

"– Yes. That's correct."

Debs bursts out laughing. She says: "Russell! That's a whopping lie! How can you even say that?"

"*Silence!*" Dame Davina snarls. There is a line… There *must* be a line. Shoutouts from the Everyday Benches *cannot be tolerated*… Even so, Dame Davina hesitates to speak again. She glowers at Debs, daring her to continue. Luckily, it seems Debs has nothing to add.

"But they must have returned the phone to you very quickly?" Lord Jeremy says. "Your replies to the post are timed and dated…"

"Pardon?"

"They must have returned the phone to you very quickly," Lord Jeremy says again. "How did you get the phone back?"

"… That's correct… They threw it out the window as they were driving off."

"And yet even then you didn't call the police?" Lord Jeremy says. "At any rate, there's no call logged…"

"By that time there wasn't any point. They had

already navigated the truck from the premises. As you have correctly highlighted, I had already sent the Instagram post by the time the lorry departed. A post I very much regret… You have to understand that I did it before I fully appreciated the seriousness of the situation–"

"You've just said you were very aware of the seriousness of the situation."

"Before I appreciated the seriousness of the situation," Russell reiterates, stubbornly, "I posted the image because Ozias Plume seemed like a really nice person. Very down to earth. Also, don't forget, he was the most famous individual in the world. And there he was, in Plumtree Court, Reading, Berkshire, UK. I could not resist… On the other hand, *he* suggested the selfie, if memory serves. We posed for the selfie together. He took the photograph and handed me back the phone. As I say it was before I knew… a lot of things… I felt very foolish afterwards. You can probably imagine."

THE POST

Two men, heads touching, one grinning, the other, with an unusually shiny face, looking off camera, apparently talking to someone.

Russell took the pic. His outstretched arm is clearly visible. Just before he took it, Ozias called out to Debs: *Debs, Russell wants to take a selfie with me, but I think it's a bit weird. Are you going to tell him…*

Russell, dizzy with reflected fame at that point, didn't hear, or didn't listen. He put his arm around Ozias and beamed and snapped and posted.

It all happened while Debs was fiddling with levers on the juggernaut dashboard, in search of a lever that might open up the back doors. If she'd noticed what was happening, she would have discouraged Russell, who at that point didn't fully appreciate not simply the seriousness of the situation, but any aspect of the situation at all. It would be humiliating for him when he found out. No lover would knowingly post an image of themselves, grinning like a starstruck nincompoop, arm in arm with their usurper.

Beneath the post, Russell had written: Having a nice chat with Ozias Plume! (I kid you not!!!!) and beneath that, various tags: #ozias #oziasplume #lorries #surprise #celebritymeetup #readingcity #orchardlane #bounce #bouncebounce #magicpotion

All of which leaves several questions unanswered.

Not that this matters to anyone, really – except Russell, who is keen to clear his name; or maybe just keen to have his voice heard before he dies; or for Debs to realise- for Debs to know – for her to notice…

Russell is too frightened to visit the doc. But he feels that he may be dying – and that there is something missing in the life he has led until this point: an enormous hole which fills his skin and seeps out of his skin through his pores. He longs to fill this unfillable hole. In the meantime, there are the questions – the only questions of any genuine interest to this Ad Hoc Non Statutory Public Inquiry:

What happened to the lorry full of lotion?

What was in the lotion?

Also– how did smarmy Nicholas James, lately knighted, get his fists on so much of it, what did he do with it once he got it, how much money did he make, and why hasn't he been arrested?

In the grand scheme of the story, it's a small piece: Russell's Instagram post, and the message beneath it from his former brother-in-law, Barry DeLuxe-Kelson.

Dame Davina and Lord Jeremy want to move on from Russell's evidence now. Russell has denied the lorry was bouncing, which is excellent. Other than that, he's not proving to be tremendously helpful: nobody believes a word he says.

Sir Nicholas James has agreed to give evidence via video link tomorrow morning and Barry DeLuxe-Kelson has agreed to appear in person.

Lord Jeremy, Dame Davina, Russell Drisell and

all the sardines in the VP Box can only hope that civilisation will survive until then.

THE OTHER VERSION

Ozias was in the driving seat. Debs was beside him. Russell stood on the tarmac, looking up at them. The engine was running. Debs said: "Russell, there's a whole lot of stuff I haven't told you yet, and some of it's going to make you very unhappy, and I am so sorry. But we have to go – we need to get this lorry somewhere. We have a lot to do. Do you understand?"

He did not.

She said, "Russell, we have to go together, now, all three of us, so I can explain things to you, and so you can understand. The lorry is full of this amazing… It's something magical, Russell – you won't believe it until you try it. But it makes everything clear. Literally…" She considered this enormous statement. "Or at least - it makes everything as clear as it ever needs to be." She grinned. Couldn't stop herself. "… And," she added, "it makes everything funny."

He looked at her as if she was mad. Also, his phone was buzzing. She was talking rubbish, and his phone was buzzing.

Debs waited, Ozias waited, the juggernaut's engine rumbled. Somebody was walking along the tarmac towards them. Somebody was shouting at them from one of the windows above. Somebody was going to call the police.

Russell said nothing. He put a hand to his cheek: toothache incoming. He noticed that. A nasty toothache.

"… Think of anything…" Debs was saying. "… literally, anything! And you suddenly realise it's OK. That is –" Unfortunately she started laughing. Ozias did too. "Of course it's not OK – 'anything' isn't OK - but it is OK. Because… what else can it be? It is what it is. *Do you understand?"*

Russell did not.

"It is what it is," she said again. How could he not understand that? But he didn't appear to. He just stood there, scowling at her. "Please, Russell. Get in the lorry. We have to go. Now. We have to go now…" Unfortunately, she was still laughing.

Ozias said: "Russell – we need to get out of here. Come with us. Please. Debs will explain everything."

Russell backed away. (Clutching his mobile, Your Honour, which at that instant was aglow with notifications.)

The approaching figure was getting close. And now there was another one, coming from the opposite side of the building. And above them, several foreheads were poking out of windows. Debs, Ozias, Russell and the Lorry had been on the tarmac, making a racket, for more than twenty minutes. But now the lorry had settled, and figures were popping up everywhere. They were approaching from all angles.

Ozias said it one more time: "Russell, we have to go. Come with us now. Otherwise we can come back and get you tomorrow, if you like. Seriously ... I am so sorry. I am. But we need to go."

Russell clutched his cheek. His tooth felt as if it might explode. All he could think about was the tooth. He couldn't speak. He stood there, nursing his tooth. Ozias paused for a couple more seconds he edged the lorry forward. Waited. Russell didn't move. Slowly Ozias edged the lorry further forward, then a little further, then he didn't stop.

"Russell, I'm coming back for you!" Debs shouted out the window. "I'm coming back tomorrow!"

Russell couldn't speak. His tooth was agony.

The lorry departed.

Angry figures surrounded him.

He collapsed onto the tarmac, in too much pain to speak.

And in the morning, the lorry was gone, Debs was gone, the toothache was gone. He was tucked up in his bed, and Debs, he supposed, was not in bed beside him because she was in the bathroom. He wondered if he'd dreamed it all – until he checked his mobile and he opened up his

Instagram.

He took the day off work – obviously. Debs came round at lunchtime and told him their relationship was over. She brought some of the lotion, but he wouldn't touch it. She left it for him, open, on the kitchen table. He wore rubber gloves to wash it all down the sink, and he put the jar into recycling.

But he didn't lose out completely. Someone - Ozias Plume - had wired a million pounds to his bank account.

Russell didn't dream that.

The *NEWSPAPER*

NEW HOPE
FOR
LAUGHING SICKNESS

Special report by our science correspondent

Kitty Manage

DAY FOUR

… There are similar reports in the usual outlets. The world of shared-values is finding something to be hopeful about this morning.

Actually, on closer examination, the new hope isn't terribly hopeful after all. Nevertheless, Lord Jeremy is pleased to read the piece as he is chauffeured in from Islington this morning. It sends out, he feels, a positive message, while also highlighting the extreme seriousness of the situation.

Apparently, according to Kitty Manage, scientists are on the brink of discovering an antidote. In the meantime, readers are reminded to be 'hyper alert' to symptoms:

- Inappropriate laughter
- Impulsive, irresponsible, ill-conceived 'generosity'
- An ability to stand very still for extended periods
- Potentially unhygienic and unsafe work attire
- Bendy feet
- Waxy 'death mask' skin
- Casual approach to rules and regulations
- A tendency to ignore official fines
- A loss of interest in shopping

All well and good, Kitty Manage reminds her readers. Some of the above may on first glance appear innocuous – even quite welcome. But these early symptoms quicky develop, leading to a loss of social and personal ambition (often and most obviously evidenced, Kitty says, by sufferers' 'ill-matched clothing and scruffy attire'); a loss of interest in public and current affairs; and an unwillingness to spend more than a few minutes at a time in front of a computer screen…

"And yes, this may sound rather amusing - especially to those already afflicted," Kitty Manage chides. "But the sight of scruffily attired people, young and old, rolling about on pavements, often helpless with laughter, flouting regulations and possibly refusing to pay fines, will ultimately cost us all. Mental health experts believe that exhibiting disdain for the shared values of modern life are a key factor when developing sociopathic personality disorders, which will lead initially leading to personal ruin, and, ultimately to total societal breakdown."

Over the last few weeks, Kitty's readers have read this many times before. Not that it stops them wanting to read it again.

In any case, the 'New Hope' touted at the top of the piece turns out to be a damp squib. The meat of the matter is this:

Scientists still haven't the faintest idea what

causes the disorder, how it spreads, where it comes from, what it is, or how it can be cured. They know next to nothing. But they are clear that what they do know, isn't good. There is growing evidence, for example, that the Silly Sickness (as the media has named it) may lead to early onset dementia, obesity, anxiety, depression, and incontinence. Readers are reminded, once again, that they must be 'hyper alert' around contagion triggers: public spaces, drinking fountains, human touch – and so on.

On the brighter side, Kitty reports: recreational shopping has been shown to boost production of haploid delta-gametes D12.f chromo-splimatic B-cells. Which are known to inhibit infection. The public is being encouraged to shop. But to shop from home. Follow these government guidelines, Kitty says, and we should all be ok.

To make things easier, Kitty adds, the government has come up with a handy acronym. Everyday people should be asking themselves:

F– Is my **F**unny really funny?
S – Am I being **S**ensible?
A – Am I taking care to **A**void trigger contagion points?
R – Should I **R**eport this laughter incident?

F-S-A-R.

No mention of the government's Ad Hoc Non Statutory Public Inquiry in Kitty's article, Lord Stevens of Dirkmass and Stirton notes. The shared-values brigade don't have much time for Ozias and his preposterous stories. They try their best to pretend he doesn't exist, which is difficult because on the World Wide Web, as previously mentioned, Ozias Plume is King.

In any case Lord Jeremy is pleased to note that on Page 5, there's an article informing readers that Ozias Plume's father changed his name and fled to the Costa Del Crime, after being suspected of sexual misconduct [a clever add-on, thanks to Dame Davina's wily but irrelevant question] and a series of failed armed robberies.

The report, by "a Newspaper journalist" has been lifted word-for-word from the information sheet Lord Stevens of Dirkmass and Stirton delivered to the VP Box yesterday lunchtime after he'd switched off their speakers.

As his limousine draws up to the front steps of the building with the boring room inside it, Lord Jeremy closes his newspaper. He leans back, and he breaths.

Not everything has gone to the dogs, then. Not yet.

Even so, there is something he needs to do before questioning Sir Nicholas. He was going to do it anyway - of course. Sir Nicholas's bossy WhatsApp this morning had been quite unnecessary.

39

He calls Ozias Plume back to the hot seat.

Lord Stevens wants to ask him, in a loud and clear voice, and with the VP mics very much switched to 'ON':

"Mr Plume, perhaps you would explain to us why you saw fit to deposit one million pounds into Mr Drisell's bank account the day after you met him? It seems a remarkably generous gesture."

Ozias, shiny from breakfast, shiny all over, unendurably springy, almost floating in his seat - doesn't answer at once. He shimmers with good nature, but his massive brain is in a confused state. He is attempting to understand the question within Lord Jeremy's question. For all his massive brains he can't see it yet. He says: "Well… because I wanted to?"

Lord Stevens of Dirkmass chuckles. "Perhaps you were hoping for something in exchange?"

Ozias Plume stares at Lord Jeremy. He says: "Oh. Is this why you called me back to the hot seat?"

Lord Jeremy feels a shock of irritation. It's amazing: very physical. *He fucking hates this man.* He raises one of his dusty eyebrows (an old trick) and says: "Apparently so."

Ozias is flummoxed: "But what would I have wanted in exchange?"

Lord Jeremy says: "His silence, perhaps."

"- About what?"

Lord Jeremy isn't certain, now that he asks. Why would Ozias Plume want silence? He's been broadcasting his fatuous ideas about magic lotions from every available roof top, for the past three months. Lord Jeremy says: "… You stole his girlfriend."

A beat while this lands.

F.S.A.R. … FSAR … *FSAR!*

And then everyone laughs. Everyone, pretty much, except for a sprinkling of security wagglers, and Dame Davina, who looks livid, and Sideline Su, who hasn't caught up, and the useful-idiot super-wagglers in the VP Box, who aren't very good listeners and who never laugh unless they're told to.

Ozias says: "I sent him the money because I felt bad for him… Russell is very set in his ways, and I thought – well, he doesn't want to be free. He's too afraid to be free. That's a terrible thing, my Lordship. Don't you think?"

His Lordship does not think anything of the kind. He raises another dusty eyebrow. "So, you gave him a million pounds, because he didn't want to be free?"

Ozias thinks about it. "When you put it like that

it does seem a bit silly," he says, "At the time, it seemed to be the least worst option." Ozias shrugs. "Anyway – he didn't ask for it, and I'm pretty sure he never said thank you. But I should say – I'm grateful to him, because thanks to his Instagram post, which I know he regrets– he gave us Barry DeLuxe-Kelson, and Barry gave us Nicholas James, and Nicholas… Well, as you know, Nicholas was the game changer. At least I *think* he was… He's tremendously secretive, but I assume he made a lot of money out of it… On the other hand, who really knows? Everything's gone so crazy this past week or so…" He laughs. His gesture is a vague one. It encompasses everything, all around him, going crazy. He says: "It's a mystery, the way things are going. I don't have the answers."

Dame Davina jumps in. "You do not have the answers, Mr Plume, I am grateful to you for highlighting that. And I should add, it's not for you to comment on Sir Nicholas's financial arrangements. Sir Nicholas has repeatedly stated that he made no money out of any of this… fiasco. This is a matter of public record. And so, I would ask you to retract that last comment, Mr Plume, or you may well have a lawsuit on your hands."

Under the panellist desk, Lord Jeremy's dry palm reaches across to Dame Davina's gargantuan thigh. He squeezes it. Or a portion of it. As much as his small, dry hand can grasp. He is grateful to her. *Thank you*, says the little hand. *Thank you for being an adult in the room*.

But Dame Davina is not impressed. She swivels her face towards him and glares. Lord Jeremy snatches his hand away.

THE WEATHER IN NORFOLK

It's a sunny day in Norfolk. A beautiful, sunny day. Barry DeLuxe-Kelson has been up since five, doing useful and practical things, and now he's walking through the country lanes towards a large village, and a small but, lately, exorbitantly popular supermarket, where he works as cashier and chief sachet dispenser, four-and-a-half days a week.

Actually, he's just stopped in his tracks. He is standing very still, staring at the hedge. He's fully engaged in one of Ozias Plumes' previously identified favourite pass times. He's watching a couple of butterflies flapping around each other, and he's wondering what the dynamic is: if they're arguing or flirting or if it's something else, unclassifiable.

Butterflies.

And then his mobile rings, disturbing the butterflies and disturbing him.

He remembers he's meant to be in London this morning, explaining his role in bringing civilisation to its brink. So - he looks at the phone, ringing away in its humourless fashion, and he wonders whether to pick up. He ought to pick up. *Should he pick up?* He doesn't want to: he can feel all sorts of bad vibes coming off that little machine... Perhaps he should do what Ozias did and throw the wretched thing into the beautiful landscape. On the other hand, he needs it. Also, he can't afford to buy another. Never wants to buy another. Also, also, also – here's the crux: Barry DeLuxe-Kelson gave his word. Ha. Imagine that. He said he'd talk at the wretched Inquiry. They're relying on him. And who knows? *(Who knows?)* Maybe he can help.

He picks up.

"Hello!!" he cries. Bright and breezy. It irritates his caller.

THE WINDFALL

Until two months ago, when he lost interest in current affairs altogether, Barry DeLuxe-Kelson, unlike his ex-brother-in-law Russell Drisell, drew his understanding of developments in the wider world from all sorts of alternative news sources. And so, at the time of Russell Drisell's infamous Instagram post, Barry was aware of a lot of stuff that Russell Drisell absolutely, most definitely, was not. He was aware, for example, of Ozias Plume's Damascene moment in Mexico, because he followed Ozias Plume on the social network platform that Ozias himself owned. Ozias had been using his platform to bang on about magical Mexican potions for a couple of weeks before the night of the great #bounce. Millions of people were talking about it: just no one in Russell's orbit. So when Russell, dizzy with reflected fame, posted the selfie with Ozias beside him, the juggernaut behind him, and the hashtag regarding magic potions, Barry DeLuxe-Kelson thought to himself –

Well blow me down! Maybe there's something in this for me… Why not?

Barry's a chancer – or he was. An opportunist. Not a crook, exactly, but someone with one eye on the ball no matter what, and a sharp antennae for sitting ducks. The proverb about fools and their money being quickly parted might have been invented with Barry in mind. He'd be the one engineering the parting. Barry DeLuxe-Kelson, despite his silly name, which he changed by deed poll for a bet during a short stint at university, is nobody's fool.

The reason he follows Russell Drisell on Instagram: he was very briefly married to Russell's sister, Holly. He and Holly, who have one child together, are on much better terms these days – especially since he gave her the entirety of his unexpected windfall.

42

In any case, Sir Nicholas isn't due to begin his video evidence for another hour, and it's becoming increasingly obvious that if this Ad Hoc Non Statutory Public Inquiry is to make any ground at all, some flexibility in the protocols is going to be required. Dame Davina is struggling with this. She wants to reschedule Barry DeLuxe-Kelson's evidence. He had said that he would come to the Inquiry in person, and now he's standing in a lane in Norfolk, babbling about butterflies, and insisting he can't be late for work.

"I'll walk and talk," he's saying. His voice is on speaker, belting out in the Panellists' Box, and he's being more verbose than usual because he's embarrassed to have let everyone down. He's telling them about his vegetable garden, which – in a previously unimaginable development, has become his greatest obsession. "I'm so sorry. I got side-tracked. I found butterflies eating the cabbages... were you aware they did that? They absolutely do! I realised I needed some sort of lightweight netting for the-"

"You're a gardener?" interrupts Sideline Su. She wants to manoeuvre the monologue so she can tell everyone about the time a nationally renowned TV gardener complemented her on her green fingers, after she'd shown him a photograph of some roses her gardener had planted. But she can't remember the TV gardener's name, which is disconcerting. Tuckbridge?

Also, she realises, in a blinding flash, the roses had not actually been grown by her. They'd been grown by the gardener, Jerry. So it was Jerry with the green fingers, not Su!

Su chortles at her extreme silliness – she's quite shocked to notice it. And the chortle comes out louder than she expects. It comes out in a great, unwelcome guffaw.

"I admit it! I haven't got green fingers!" she exclaims.

Lord Jeremy and Dame Davina turn. They stare.

Sideline Su continues to laugh. She takes a breath. She wipes a tear away. She says: "My gardener, *Jerry,* has wonderful green fingers." And then she starts laughing again.

"Does he?" Barry is saying, "Well perhaps he could advise me about the butterflies-"

"Oh I'm sure he could!"

Dame Davina thrums the panellists' table and glares at Su.

Sensible Su, who is about to offer Barry her gardener's contact details, notices Dame Davina's glare. "Oh dear, *listen to us*, rabbiting on!" she beams. "I apologise! Back to business! Mr DeLuxe, how about you tell the Inquiry what you can over the phone? Would you be happy with that? I'm sure someone clever will be able to patch your call into the main room so everyone can hear. It seems silly otherwise, now that we have you on the phone. And it'll save you the journey."

"It's not as simple as that. There are formalities…." (Dame Davina, obviously.)

"True," Lord Jeremy says.

"You are supposed to be present in person," Dame Davina adds.

"Yes. I'm so sorry- As I say-"

"Well but it doesn't really matter, does it?" interrupts Sensible Su. "It's convenient for Barry to stay where he is. And I don't see how it makes much difference to us, really…"

"It's not the *correct procedure*," Dame Davina says icily. She glances at Lord Jeremy, who nods gravely, in full agreement. "However," Dame Davina continues, "on this occasion…" she's about to say, *we are willing to overlook the irregularity and allow Mr DeLuxe-Kelson to continue...* But Mr DeLuxe-Kelson is continuing anyway.

He's saying: "We'll need to be quick though. I'm meant to be opening up this morning. There's always such a long queue and I don't like to keep people waiting… Shall I begin?"

THE WINDFALL cont.

They need to connect his voice to a wider sound

system, so people can hear him in the VP and boring rooms. It takes a moment to organise. He is keen to begin, and so he kicks off the moment it's done. Walking and talking.

"So I became involved as soon I spotted Russell's Insta post."

Lord Jeremy doesn't like that Barry has kicked off without first being given a Green Light. This is a formal Inquiry, with rules and etiquettes and so forth, chief among them that he (and Dame Davina, up to a point) are in charge. So he butts in. He talks over Barry. "If you could begin," he says, "by telling us how you first became involved with Mr Plume, I think we can then take it from there."

"- What?" says Barry Deluxe-Kelson, a bit flummoxed.

Laughter in the boring room (laughter in the streets. The biggest fool in England is just about to speak):

"I said, if you could begin by telling us how you first became involved with Mr Plume…"

Deluxe-Kelson giggles. "But that's what I was doing!"

Laughter in the boring room (laughter in the streets)…

Dame Davina says: "Silence!"

It doesn't work. A low, happy rumble is gathering momentum in that big, boring room. At a rough guess, 60 per cent of the everydays are chuckling now, their shoulders gently shaking. More alarming still, the security wagglers don't seem much inclined to stop them. They stand against the walls, as usual, hands crossed at the crotch, feet apart; but they don't move. *They don't move.* Also, some of them are grinning.

Dame Davina notices this. She pretends to have dropped her pen and busies herself by retrieving it. The laughter subsides.

"I'm going to rattle on through," says Deluxe-Kelson "It's probably most efficient. And then you can ask any questions at the end. All right?"

Lord Jeremy's got blood pumping round his jaw and chin, making his face feel weird and heavy. He is flushed with outrage. It is *not* 'all right'. "If you would like to go ahead and tell us what you remember," he says. "We will throw in questions as and when we see fit. Please, continue."

The everyday people in the room – at least (rough guess) about 60 per cent of them - are beginning to feel sorry for Lord Stevens of Dirkmass and Stirton. They can feel his panic rising, his pride and his pain, battling away. It's funny and it's also tragic, which makes it funnier, and more tragic still. They try to muffle their laughter.

"… So, I was lying in bed," Barry continues, "Quite an early night for me, back then. In the dark ages, as I call them…" He pauses for a hearty laugh, forgetting momentarily about his own desire to be snappy. "I was flicking through Insta... all the normal crap. And then, there was a picture of Russell with his arm around Ozias Plume, standing side by side in front of a lorry! There were a lot of hashtags. One about the lorry bouncing. Another about magic lotions... I was..."

Barry pauses. He chortles.

"There are no words to describe my surprise. None. I thought to myself *hello, hello!*

"Russell's a good bloke. But he's *slow*. He probably hasn't the faintest idea what he's handling here. At that point, I had no idea – and didn't much care - whether the so called 'magic potion' was a hoax. What I knew was that there were millions of people in the world who, like me, had heard Ozias talking about it very passionately, and who believed in it, and who believed in him. Do you see where I'm going with this?"

Lord Jeremy smirks. At last. "I think I see it clearly," he says. "You saw an unsuspecting idiot, in the shape of your ex brother-in-law, and a lorry-full of snakeskin oil, and you thought you might be able to make a fast buck, selling it to a gullible public, desperate to believe it might bring them some quote-on-quote 'happiness'. Am I right?"

"Yes!" replies Barry, joyfully. "So I contacted Russell via the post. Russell never actually replied. Who *did* reply – and this is where I think it gets interesting…"

"It's already terribly interesting!" says Sideline Su. "I use Instagram quite a bit. So I'm familiar with how it works."

"… Ok. Well, Debs Malone replied. And then, amazingly, Sir Nicholas James. Sir Nicholas James actually *DMd* me!" Barry pauses to laugh. "The King of the Snake Oil salesmen himself. So-"

Dame Davina says: "Mr DeLuxe-Kelson. Please retract that previous comment."

But Mr DeLuxe-Kelson continues. "I often wondered how he ever came to see Russell's post. Perhaps he was lying in bed, a bit bored, scrolling through Instagram, just like I was, and he came upon it via one of its hashtags. #bounce maybe…" He chuckles. "Anyway, I messaged him back right away… I had no idea what I was actually selling, or even if I was in a position to sell it. But in those days that sort of thing didn't tend to stop me." Another burst of laughter, very merry. "*I* blagged. *Sir Nicholas* blagged. We came to an agreement."

"Hang on a mo.," says Sideline Su. "What was Sir Nicholas blagging about? And if you don't mind me asking, why did Sir Nicholas think someone like you could be of any help to him?"

"But he was quite right! I *could* help him!" Barry replies. There is joy and humour in his voice. "Sir Nicholas and I helped each other very much. Sir Nicholas, being Snake Oil King, did not want to be directly involved, for obvious reasons-"

"Hang on a mo.," says Sideline. "What reasons?"

Barry hesitates. He's embarrassed. Is she an idiot? Or is she teasing him? He settles, incorrectly, on the latter option, and it colours his response. "Hahaha - well, obviously," he says, "Sir Nicholas James is not the sort of guy who wants it advertised he's bulk buying untested magical lotions off the back of a lorry - literally," he adds as an afterthought. "On the other hand, he *is* the sort of guy who'd be more than happy to make a lot of money out of untested magical lotions bulk-bought off the back of a lorry... And Sir Nicolas has tentacles. *Amazing* tentacles." Barry laughs. "That guy can shift anything, anywhere, and nobody's going to ask questions. He can get away with stuff the rest of us can't."

Lord Jeremy has been waiting, biting his tongue. He had imagined that Dame Davina might already have put a stop to this river of mal/mis/ and/or disinformation - but for some reason she's not saying anything. Why? He doesn't know. She's looking down at her notes, scribbling away, with her miserable, tiny handwriting. What the hell is wrong with her? He doesn't want to be the one publicly defending Nicholas. It wouldn't look good. Nevertheless, he can't let this dreadful man jabber on indefinitely. Also, he realises– *Jesus Christ*–

He leans across and switches off the VP speakers.

He can do that, at least. He watches and waits to see the response from inside the box… They glance up at the sound system and back down at their notes. Pick up their phones. Nothing much.

"… Oh ok," Sideline is saying, "Gotcha. Sorry to interrupt! Carry on!"

Barry can't remember where he was. "Where was I?" he asks.

"You were slandering a much respected member of the establishment; a man with an unblemished reputation, recently knighted by his Majesty the King for his services to the nation… I suggest we move on," snaps Lord Jeremy.

Rumbles of laughter in the room. All over the room.

Dame Davina knows better than to look up from her squiggly notes.

Lord Jeremy feels the blood in his ears. *What are they laughing about? What's so fucking funny?* "I'm glad you're all so amused," he says. "I don't suppose you'll be laughing when the lawsuit arrives on your doormat."

Who is he talking to? Are the people on the Everyday Benches likely to receive lawsuits for laughing*? Or just fines? Both or neither? He's not thinking straight. He's not thinking at all! Anyway, he doesn't* like *it here anymore. His fellow panellists are idiots, and Dame Davina is an eyesore. Nobody has to be that fat...* For reasons he doesn't analyse, he wishes he was at home with his dog, Brutus, and a nice soft pillow over his head.

"That's it," says Barry. "I was explaining why Sir Nicholas - of the unblemished reputation..." he chuckles "... didn't want to be seen anywhere near the product. He offered me £100,000 up front and he put me in touch with a couple of people to help with the logistics. And, basically, I sort of took it from there...

"Ozias and Debs kept back half to distribute themselves. Which was difficult for us because, as I said to Sir Nicholas, they were *giving* it away while we were trying to *sell* it.... On the flip side they were quite hindered by Ozias' recognisability. He couldn't go anywhere without being mobbed, which meant Debs was doing a lot of the heavy lifting. Meanwhile, we were marketing it as a party drug. Or a health supplement. Both. Same packaging, different pitch. We labelled it X as in 'Forbidden' for the partygoers. X as in 'Kiss-Kiss' for the health bods. Whatever. We sold it anywhere we could, frankly. And of course, as the word spread, my job got easier. The thing developed a momentum of its own, and now we're at the point where, frankly, it doesn't matter how it's labelled or who pays for it or doesn't-"

Lord Jeremy guffaws. "Are you seriously attempting to suggest," he says, "that your and Plume's haphazard dispensation of variously labelled *little cream sachets* around Greater London... has single handedly brought us to this national crisis? Are you really trying to claim that?"

Barry DeLuxe thinks Lord Jeremy is being quite rude. He says, "You've forgotten Debs. She was the brains and the brawns, really."

Lord Jeremy sneers. He's sneering so hard it's pulling at his cheeks and upsetting his diction. He laughs. It's a genuine laugh, full of viciousness. "You, Prume and Mz Marone! Huhhuhhhh... Our very own Free Muskadeers!"

"Muskadeers?" repeats Barry.

"Assurd!" declares Lord Jeremy. He's stopped laughing. There's nothing to laugh about anyway. His ears are throbbing with fury. He wants to thump the table. He wants to thump it so hard it smashes under his papery fist. "Really. I can't risten to this nonsense much ronger."

Dame Davina glances at him. She leans into the mic: "I would agree with Lord Stevens. It's a fairly preposterous statement. Indeed, a dangerous one. Is this really what you are claiming, Mr Deluxe-Kelson?"

No reply.

"Mr DeLuxe-Kelson? Can you hear me?"

Still, no reply.

"Mr DeLuxe-Kelson!" says Dame Davina, as imperially as she can.

"… What turned it, I think…" Barry says at last. And then he pauses again. It's a long pause, and it takes a while for people to realise that he's laughing. He's laughing helplessly. He's thought of something so funny he cannot find the breath to share it yet.

Is my Funny really Funny?

Probably not.

Either way, laughter is infectious, and people are joining in. Soon, the room is full of laughter, and no one really knows why. Gales of laughter rise from the Everyday Benches. And now the wagglers can't contain themselves, either. Upstairs in their airconditioned VP Box, the super-wagglers look down on the everydays in bewilderment and fear.

The people's laughter makes the walls bulge. And the bulging walls make the people laugh even more.

"The walls are bulging!" Debs cries, pointing at the walls - and laughing. "Or am I seeing things? *The walls are bulging!"*

They are, too. Even Lord Stevens of Dirkmass and Stirton can see it.

"… What turned it, I think," Barry is saying, once again. His voice echoes across the room. He can't see the walls bending. He can't see the havoc his laughter has created. He's trying to pull himself together. "What really turned it was Sir Nicholas getting the terrors and ordering us to dump everything into the Tham-

"ENOUGH!" roars Lord Stevens. He's going to clear the room.

ONE MONTH AGO

Sir Nicholas James sat alone at his Oxfordshire dining table, on pleasure-maximising automatic. He was eating a boiled egg and reading the FT.

Toast - would be good. He moved an arm toward the toast, which was well within reach. Also butter and marmalade.

Slow crunch.

His second wife was doing something with the horses. His two younger children (from the second wife) were away at school.

Crunch.

The driver was taking him into town in 45 mins. He had a lunch at the Wolseley with–

Etc etc.

Drum roll for Sir Nicholas James!

He's 56 years old.

He's 6'3".

He's handsome. Very handsome.

Ladies can't get enough of him.

He's funny, charming, and good at everything in the world: backgammon, flyfishing, racy jokes, classical history, cunnilingus, real tennis and of course, above all, making money.

There's a piece of him missing, though. Quite a big one. It's not that he's cruel. It's that he lacks an iota of kindness. No empathy. No sympathy. Nothing. Nothing in Sir Nicholas's mind or body functions except for its own gratification. He might have taken a bath in the laughing lotion and it wouldn't have had any effect, because he is sealed. From all goodness, he is fully sealed. From himself, he is fully sealed. It's a sad state of affairs.

So there he sat, at his dining table: a lifetime of pleasure behind him, and not a moment of joy. The butler - wittily, he employed a butler - stepped softly across the hardwood floor to tell his master that the Prime Minister was on the telephone.

Sir Nicholas swallowed his marmalade, cleared his throat, uncrossed his long legs and glanced at the proffered phone. It was annoying of the Prime Minister to call during breakfast, and he considered, fleetingly, telling the butler to tell the Prime Minister he would call back. He decided against it.

"Steven!" he said. His tongue was wrenching wholemeal nuggets from between his teeth. "Early call! What can I do for you?"

... Drum roll for the Prime Minister!

Or maybe not a drum roll. Maybe a brief tap on a small tub of margarine.

Tappety-tap. Attention, please.

Steven Yallop has plodded his path direct from Wagglerland, but he claims to have plodded from much further.

It's been one of the most relentless and least inspiring plods in the history of Western civilisation. And yet here is, plodding on.

Never an act that hasn't led expediently to the next.

Never an idea that didn't emerge expediently from the last.

Never a thought that wasn't born and didn't suffocate, sealed and safe, inside one margerine tub or another.

Plod. Plod. Plod. His meaty body, his wooden face, his dead-eyed gaze, his boring turn of phrase, his monotonal, nasal voice, his tidy hair, his extraordinary stubbornness, his total absence of humour or imagination… have worked a charm, somehow. Eventually people yield to him, if only to move the project along.

Patience, Steven Yallop says to his children (whom he loves very much) *Patience and perseverance win the day.*

Steven wasn't sounding as wooden as usual this morning, Sir Nicholas noted. He was sounding concerned. Worse than that, he was sounding annoyed. "What do you know," Steven began, (no 'good morning' or anything) "about this so called 'laughing lotion' I keep hearing about? What is it exactly?"

"'Laughing lotion'?" Nicholas repeated seamlessly.

"Toby went to a festival at the weekend."

Toby is the Prime Minister's 15 year-old son, but the Prime Minister doesn't need to explain that.

"How nice for him," Nicholas said, fiddling with his egg spoon, knowing there was worse to come. "Did he have fun?"

"He came back last night."

"… Right-oh…"

A long silence. Steven Yallop often leaves them. Long, plodding silences while his cogs turn. This silence was different. Nicholas sensed it.

"He came back last night and I can tell you, he's been *babbling* ever since," the Prime Minister burst out. "Babbling like a hyena. No one can get a word of sense out him. We think he's got hold of this 'laughing' lotion. *What is it?* I'm told you're involved in it, and I can't say I'm surprised. What the bloody hell are you peddling, Nicholas? Do you have any idea?"

Nicholas took a moment. He reached one of his languorous arms for the coffee cup. Swallowed. After a while he said: "Do hyenas babble?"

The Prime Minister took a calming breath. "You're being facetious," he observed, a little more calmly.

"I wasn't," Nicholas replied. "I'm genuinely interested."

"I will ask you one more time. Do you know about this substance?"

"What substance?"

Prime Minister Steven Yallop lost it. He lost his cool. "I don't fucking know, do I?" he yelled. "If I *knew* I wouldn't be asking. It's some bullshit emanating from the Plume empire, where else?..."

The Prime Minister took another calming breath.

And for a brief moment it helped. "Plume," he said, sounding more like himself, "is clearly struggling with some mental health issues. This we already know..." But then his voice started to rise again. "And that's all very well. I'm sorry to hear it, I suppose. Or maybe I couldn't care less. *My son is sick*. We need to stop him. Whatever it is he's doing, whatever it is he's handing out to people, he needs to *stop*. WHERE THE FUCK IS HE?"

"Ozias Plume?"

"Are you in communication with him?"

"*Plume?* Absolutely not!"

"Toby tells me this laughing lotion is pretty much everywhere. But what is it? Does anyone know? Is it real? *Nobody seems to know*! All I know is, Toby has turned into a giggling simpleton overnight. He was normal on Friday. And now… The whole world is going mad, Nicholas! And my son is sick! *And people keep fucking laughing!*"

"I'm sorry," Nicholas said, sounding not sorry at all. "I wish I could help. I really do. I wish I knew what you were even talking about."

"Is there an antidote? Are you aware of an antidote?" bawled the Prime Minister, normally so wooden. "I'm telling you now, Nicholas-" at the other end of the line, Steven Yallop stamped his solid trotter, making a small dent in the 300-year old marble floor beneath him. "I'm making it ILLEGAL. As of today. Anyone caught using it, handling it – even fucking *speaking* about it… goes to jail. Straight to jail. And that includes you. Do you understand?"

"Steven, really, I wish I had the faintest idea what –"

"DO YOU UNDERSTAND? Tell me you understand! I want to hear you say it. Say, *'yes, Prime Minster, I understand!'*"

… But that wasn't quite the way Sir Nicholas rolled. He preferred to choose his own words. He kept quiet.

"SAY IT!" roared the plodder.

Sir Nicholas said, "Absolutely, Prime Minister. One hundred per cent. Understood."

The Prime Minister hung up. He was extremely annoyed.

45

And now so was Sir Nicholas.

He was a man very good at covering his tracks. Rather, he'd become the sort of man whose tracks were no longer much scrutinised, due to all the other filth that would be uncovered in the process. He was invulnerable. Unassailable, he used to tell himself in the mirror. Untouchable, until the day they find him hanging from a bedsheet in a New York correctional centre, with the video surveillance on the blink. Haha. Nicholas James rather liked that joke. It made him feel important.

Anyway, he was off his breakfast now.

He called DeLuxe-Kelson, in Norfolk, who was frying bacon and eggs.

"Hey," said Nicholas, brusque and disagreeable. There was still a nugget of wholemeal stuck between his back teeth. He wanted to go straight in, as the PM had, but by the time his tongue returned to position Barry DeLuxe-Kelson was already launched and in full sail.

"Ah!" Barry said, "I'm glad you called. I was thinking you should probably be aware that I've decided to stop monetising. I lost the heart."

"What?"

"You've made back your initial outlay – more than. Probably ten times over. So we're clear."

"What?"

"I *said*…" Barry pronounced more slowly. "I'm not asking for money anymore. It's slowing everything down. What we really need to do is speed it up before the media goes fully off the rails and the government tries to ban it. There was a nasty little article somebody showed me yesterday. Did you see it?" Nicholas heard Barry's gusty laughter and the sound of his frying. "They were muttering about an *anti-laughter law*! Ohh, you couldn't make it up! … Seriously, though. I was thinking--"

Sir Nicholas said: "You want to *give it* away?"

"That's what Debs and Ozias have been doing since the beginning, as you know… presumably. Were you aware of that? I'm pretty sure I mentioned it. Either way you've more than recouped your money. And as I say, I've lost the hunger, Sir Nicolas... I just don't seem to care that much anymore. Know what I mean? I've got a super job at a lovely shop... And frankly, the people are coming *to me* now, so…" He laughs. "And you should see the queues! I literally don't have to do anything. There's no justification for charging people. I can't possibly charge them anymore."

Sir Nicholas takes a millisecond to absorb the relevant input, and to tune out the rest. News that Plume and his bird have been giving the stuff away for free brings with it many ramifications, all of them, on quick calibration, welcome. Above all it means that he, Sir Nicholas James, is off the hook.

"Dump it," Sir Nicholas says.

"What's that?"

"Dump it. Get rid of it. I don't care what you do with it, just get rid of it. Dump it in the river and burn the van. Get rid of everything. And send me confirmation by the end of the day."

"*Dump* it?! Are you mad?"

"The order comes direct from the Prime Minister. I want nothing more to do with it. As of now, you're one hundred per cent on your own."

As Barry washed up his frying pan, he started laughing again…

Dump it?

Dump it, indeed!

46

And now here we are, just one short month later, and civilisation is on the brink.

Lord Jeremy is on his feet, he's roaring into his microphone, ordering everyone out of the room. He's demanding someone cut off the caller, but Sensible Su is bent double with laughter and wouldn't know which button to press anyway. Dame Davina has momentarily frozen. She is rigid. She is transfixed, like a rabbit in the headlights. Her world is falling apart. And Barry DeLuxe-Kelson is still talking. He's giggling. He's saying:

…also dumped it into the two largest reservoirs … a massive one up in the Midlands and then another one on the M25…

"Cut him off!" Lord Jeremy says. "Cut him off!"

But nobody's doing anything, and in the boring room below, almost everyone is laughing.

Ozias and Debs are more than simply laughing.

They're on their feet. They're pumping the air. They're embracing everyone around them. They're leaping and dancing with joy! All this time they've been beavering away, and Barry's been beavering away – and Barry's elves, and all the elves: all of them, and all of us, we've been beavering away...

Laughter is infectious.

"The answer, my friend, is blowing in the wind," Ozias sings, as he and Debs waltz beneath the VP Box (still muted). *"The answer is blowing in the wind!!"*

Their work is almost done.

Yes, it is.

Someone, somewhere cuts the telephone line and DeLuxe-Kelson's voice is silenced. But his work, too, is done. The word is out, and the show is over.

Slowly, shambolically, the giggling masses shuffle from the boring room, back into the watery world. And Barry, realising that the line is dead, returns to his study of the butterflies.

He wonders, vaguely, if the panellists believed him about the reservoirs. He thinks maybe they did.

Not that it matters any more.

The answer, my friend, is blowing in the wind.

He laughs. And it's obvious the butterflies laugh too.

47

Dame Davina returns to her senses. She says to Lord Jeremy: "There's going to be a run on bottled water, Jeremy. We need to mitigate. We need to get the Prime Minister on the line. *Now.* And we need to seal the VP Box. Get the media some alternative information to work with."

Lord Jeremy is tapping out a message on his phone. He's sweating. He glances up at Dame Davina, a demented look in his eye. He's not heard anything she's said. He nods anyway. He presses send.

Sir Nicholas James is at that moment *en route* to his office in St James', from where he's meant to be providing his video link evidence to the Ad Hoc Non Statutory Public Inquiry. (He might just as easily have made his way to the boring room in person, of course. But it's not how Sir Nicholas rolls).

Nicholas reads the message. He says to the driver: "C*hange of plan.*"

The car makes a stately loop and heads back toward the motorway.

DAY FIVE

This morning, Dame Davina sits alone in the Panellists' Box. She has arrived very early indeed, due to the urgency of the situation. She has already spoken to replacement panellist, Trunot Salvy, who assures her he'll be with her shortly. Below her, in the boring room, a single security waggler stands all alone, waiting for the day to begin. In the meantime, Dame Davina has the newspapers... she has plenty to be getting on with:

The *NEWSPAPER*

EMERGENCY MEASURES AS SILLY SICKNESS REACHES R100+

Special report by our science correspondent

Kitty Manage

At 6pm yesterday evening, [goes the piece] *Britain's Prime Minister delivered an emergency address to the nation.*

This is actually true. In response to the extraordinary spread of the disorder, and in yet another effort to mitigate some of the 'dangerous' theories now running rampant on-line, the Prime Minister, wearing dark glasses, flanked by his Chief Medical Officer and another guy who is good at stats, stepped up to the Downing Street podium. Big moment. This is not Kitty's scoop. It's on all the front pages.

*

Yesterday morning, around the time that Lord Jeremy was urgently messaging his friend Sir Nicholas, Dame Davina took it upon herself to seize full control of the sinking ship. First, she insisted that Sensible Su be sent packing. Sensible Su was giggling so much she couldn't put up much of a defence.

"You're sick," Dame Davina told her. "You need help."

"No I'm not!" giggled Sensible Su. "I've never felt so springy. I feel fantastic!"

"Jeremy," Dame Davina turned to him. "Would you please back me up?"

He said: "Absolutely. Absolutely one hundred per cent. Su, I'm sorry but you're not well. You need to step down from the panel with immediate effect."

"*Immediate effect*," giggled Su. "Do you mean 'exactly right now'?"

Lord Jeremy gazed at her. He looked out onto the boring, and now mostly empty, room. He glanced at the VP Box, where the sound was still muted, and where the inmates were still scrolling through their Instagram. *Mineral water,* he thought to himself, in a blinding flash of light. *Buy! Buy! Buy!* He realised he needed the toilet. He said: *would you both excuse me a moment?*

And a bit like a lady on a special night out, he took his handbag with him.

*

But to return to Kitty Manage and her non-scoop. It's not her scoop, clearly. Anyone who switched on the TV last night (alarmingly few) would have known the Prime Minister had been at his podium.

The Prime Minister's appearance at the podium, not to mention the content of the message he delivered to the nation yesterday, was mostly as a result of an idea conjured up by Dame Davina and replacement panellist, Trunot Salvy. Trunot is a former Mayor of London, so quite a big cheese – or he was, once. A small man, but a big cheese (once), with a bitter face. He's been at a loose end these past couple of years, and he's always keen to be on the boards of this and that. He misses people following him down corridors, asking if he can spare a minute. So – when Davina called him with her urgent request, he was beyond delighted. Could he spare a minute? Why, *yes!* He most certainly could!

She thought of him even as she bundled Su out of the room, and Lord Jeremy was still apparently on the toilet.

Trunot Salvy was in his car, making his way over before their phone call was even finished, and it was only after they hung up that it occurred to Dame Davina that Lord Jeremy might not be coming back. Either that, or he was laying an unusually big log. *Where was he?*

So.

*

But to return to Kitty Manage and her non-scoop. The photograph on all the front pages is the same: Prime Minister Yallop and his henchmen, in a row of three, standing beneath a spanking new slogan:

GOOD BUNNIIES WEAR SUNNIES

All three men are wearing dark glasses. They look ridiculous. It's hard for a lot of people not to laugh. Anyway, according to Kitty Manage, who has skilfully merged one press release, written by Dame Davina and the new guy, Trunot Salvy, and another from Downing Street, The Science has now confirmed that infection occurs not through the air, or surface contamination, or the exchange of bodily fluids (as previously assumed) but through a lesser known energy field known as ECBW: the Eye Contact Beam-Wave. Hence the sunnies. Prime Minister Yallop, from behind his shades, has decreed that to avoid ECBW contagion, everyone of all ages must wear sunglasses at all times. Non-compliance will result in extortionate fines, pointless arrests, prison sentences and so on.

Those reporters allowed into the room with the Prime Minister were invited to ask a few sensible questions.

They wanted to know exactly how dark the sunglasses need to be, to safely evade ECBW. They didn't ask about the rumours regarding Barry DeLuxe-Kelson and contaminants in the water. The Prime Minister forestalled their curiosity on this by volunteering that The Science had confirmed the safety of UK's water supply, *as long as it was boiled pre consumption*. "As long as this vital condition is met," he said, "there is nothing whatsoever to be worried about. Pop the kettle on and have a nice cup of tea!" he said.

According to the PM, Trunot Salvy, Dame Davina, Kitty Manage and all the rest of them, stocking up on a few bottles of good ol' British mineral water was another option, should everyday people feel dehydrated; at least until the government's own brand of mineral water, *SIP-SAFE*, was up and running and ready for roll out, which it would be within days.

"In the meantime," the Prime Minister said, wrapping things up, "I'm asking us all to avoid eye contact at all times, GOOD BUNNIES WEAR SUNNIES! *Look away, save the day!*… And if you want a drink, as I say, we advise that you stick to UK mineral water, or pop the kettle on, put your feet up, and enjoy a nice cup of tea."

Hoorah.

£27 MILLION BACHELOR PAD OVERLOOKING HYDE PARK

Chak and Jacinda are – or were, until about a month ago –almost certain they had found the answer to happiness. It's still what they keep telling people, and they go around with smiles on their faces, like a couple in love. But now- here they are, sharing a *massive* bed: a bed more or less the size of Russell Drisell's open plan living area at Plumtree Court. The thrill of shagging one another in such a massive bed – or anywhere at all - was never likely to last that long, and nor has it. For Jacinda, if truth be told, the thrill was never much present in the first instance. Chak thought it was fun at first: it was fun to be shagging a notoriously beautiful woman, snatched from the arms the most interesting man in the universe, and for everyone in the whole wide world to know about it: Chak Bruton had got one over on Ozias Plume. There aren't – or there weren't – many people who could say that. Except now, Ozias has gone mad and everyone in the whole wide world knows that. Jacinda feels less like a hard-won trophy and more like a madman's sloppy seconds. Plus, obviously, for a man like Chak, it's generally more fun to be shagging nameless teenage monoglots who don't – for example – feel entitled to complain about the fen shui in his £27million bachelor pad overlooking Hyde Park.

Anyway – it's moot now. The fen shui of flat 1A, Hyde Park Tower isn't important anymore. He and Jacinda are bundling out, lickety spit. They were meant to have been giving evidence at the Ad Hoc Non Statutory Public Inquiry today, but that's out of the question, after the morning's headlines. They need (and they are united on this) to get to a place where they can feel safe. Cases of the Silly Sickness have been popping up in various corners of the globe, but Britain remains the hotspot. They need to get out of the UK.

Lickety spit.

They are not alone. London's – what Kitty Manage might refer to as "smart set" – are in panic mode this morning. On the orders of the previously obscure GHCA (Global Health Centralised Authority) in Gstaad, all commercial airlines out of UK have been grounded since this morning, and now there's a run on private jet hire. Chak, if one can believe it, is *in a queue.*

Jacinda meanwhile, like much of Kitty's 'smart set', is in a silent lather of fear and rage. For Jacinda, the situation is especially difficult. At this point she very slightly – one hundred per cent – finds Chak repulsive, for not owning a jet of his own. She's not been out with a man who didn't own his own jet for as long she can remember. Ozias had his faults, clearly. But *renting* feels very lowering, especially now, with the queue.

She's tactful enough not to give voice to the full extent of her suffering. She's aware that the situation is making Chak feel a little unmanned which, in turn, is making him disagreeable. They've spent the last several minutes side by side in that big bed, naked, except for the sunglasses, muttering bitterly over their individual news feeds.

There's a knock - tentative and apologetic. A housemaid pokes her head around the door, full of humble apologies, and wearing, as per this morning's household decree, not only sunglasses, but beneath them, for extra safety, a black scarf over her eyes. She can't really see, so she's not certain if Chak and Jacinda are in bed and within earshot. Nevertheless, she perseveres. She says:

"Sorry to disturb, Sir Madam. There is policemens waiting you. Madam. What shall I tell to them?"

Holy cow, this sends a shiver down Jacinda's spine! *Policemen?* Why? What on earth could they possibly have to say to her?

"I'm in *bed* for god's sake!" she says. "What am I supposed to do? Get out of bed and speak to them?"

Chak keeps his eyes on his newsfeed. "Probably, old chum," he says.

A moment, while Jacinda registers this.

"Do *not,*" she snarls, (her rage and fear now fully directed at him) "Repeat, do *not ever* call me 'chum'."

"Sorry, chum," he mutters. He thinks he's being funny. Or maybe he thinks that. "Maria, Jacinda needs her thingy – in the bathroom. She can't speak to the coppers in the nuddy!"

"Yes Madam Sir," says Maria. She stumbles along, pressing her hands to the bedroom walls for guidance, until she reaches the bathroom. In the bathroom, she peeks out from beneath the safety blindfold, grabs the thingy (the dressing gown) carries it back to Jacinda and almost, very nearly, falls onto the bed.

Jacinda gives an irritable yelp, takes the gown. "Thank you Maria. Please tell the policeman I will be out in a moment."

"Yes Madam. Sorry-sorry." Maria fumbles back to the door, via the walls, and exits softly.

50

Jacinda takes her time. When she finally emerges, she finds two uniformed officers at the door, both in the requisite eyewear. They've come because they're looking for Ozias and they think Jacinda might have an idea where to find him.

They've come to the wrong place. Jacinda can't help them even if she wants to; and right now, with the airplane shortage situation, she's not sure she wants to. Better to be in Ozias' good books, if possible. He might help her. He might take pity, for old time's sake. Or something.

One of the officers seems to have lost the power of speech. A few moments in, after Jacinda has graciously, charmingly, deferentially informed them both of her uselessness regarding the matter in hand, the non-speaking policeman makes an unfortunate noise: it's a cough and a fart, all in one.

Jacinda freezes, mid word.

He's been staring at the knot on the belt of her dressing gown; watching it, really, obligingly knotted, keeping the show on the road. The knot is unendurably funny. But then, so is the rug behind the door, all laid out flat, to look nice. *Somebody put it there to look flat and nice.*

He's staring at his feet. His mouth is contorting. His shoulders are shaking.

Astonishment all round.

And then a gurgle escapes from the other policeman, too.

Jacinda steps back.

"Sorry, Madam," sniggers Officer 2.

It doesn't help. "Get the fuck out of here!" she says, all charm and deference gone. "Get out!" She slams the door on them. She rushes to her wet room, and scrubs, and ventilates hyperly, and scrubs. Also, which is unusual, because Jacinda is nothing if not tough – she bursts into tears. Civilisation is on the brink.

She's never felt so afraid.

PLUMTREE COURT

Fortunately for Russell Drisell, the police service personnel that call on him at Plumtree Court have not yet – apparently - been infected with the Silly Disease. These personnel are still very serious. In this encounter, nobody farts and nobody giggles.

Russell hasn't been into work since he returned from giving evidence at the Ad Hoc Non Statutory Public Inquiry, two days ago. He's sick. Very sick. He's only left his living unit once, to buy bread and milk, and those are sitting on the kitchen counter now, growing stale and sour. He's in pain. He has a fever. Above all, he has the terrors. He's dying, and he knows it, and yet he cannot call a doctor. The moment he does that, he feels, it won't be his secret anymore. His life and death will be something real.

When the buzzer goes and he discovers, via bedside video intercom, that it's two officers of the law (in sunglasses) awaiting him, he is glad to let them in. They might be the only people in the world he wants to see right now. Except for Debs. Then again, just thinking about Debs gives him a stab of pain: a different kind of pain to the physical pain he feels all the time – better, but worse, but better. In any case he's lonely. He drags himself into the kitchen-diner-living space. He invites the policemen in, and he makes them a cup of tea.

He's wearing a pair of ski goggles, never previously used. He'd thought, one day, long years ago, at the height of his astonishing partnership with Debs, that they might, one day do something dashing together: for example, skiing. It never happened. Debs wasn't really interested, not being the athletic type, and Russell couldn't afford it. The goggles had been bought as a little joke between them, *just in case.* He didn't own sunglasses anyway. They made him feel self-conscious. When the video intercom buzzed, he was in a lot of pain, but the goggles, thankfully, were within easy reach.

*

Things are in a sorry state, he and the policemen agree. They shake their heads and sip their boiled tea and the two policemen wonder, quietly, what it is that's wrong with Russell and whether it's infectious. He looks terrible. They feel a mixture of pity and fear – and curiosity, too. It's well documented that Russell was given a million pounds by the most famous man in the world. How, they wonder, is he spending it? It doesn't seem to have made him any happier.

"Do you believe it's in the water as well as in the eyebeams?" the first policeman asks, after a pause. "What are they calling it now? EBCW... ECBW something..."

Russell says: "Possibly." Behind the goggles, his eyes are gazing miserably at his thumbs.

"It's what a lot of people are saying, after yesterday," says the other policeman, whose name is Sean. "Then there's the chap who says he put it in the reservoirs... Is that true? Are they saying it's true? I must say, it's hard to know what to believe."

"We certainly can't believe everything we see on the internet," says the one who isn't named Sean.

"But it makes you wonder... for example myself and my partner, Annie, we only drink hot beverages and fizzies at home. I'm thinking maybe that's why we're ok." He gestures his other partner, Sean. They've already discussed this. Everyone in the country has discussed it by now: "Sean's the same.

Sean and his family never drink the water."

"We don't. My wife and I find tap water a bit unpleasant to the taste, which is rather fortunate as it turns out... Who knew?... Then again our thirteen-year-old drinks gallons of the stuff. She can't get enough of it. And yet she's not infected either. We think it's because she's someone who doesn't tend to *look* at people. If you know what I mean. She's always looking at her phone!"

Russell says: "Maybe it depends on the person. Maybe some people have to drink more water to get it? Whereas, in the meantime, most people are transmitting with the ECBWs..."

The officers nod sagely.

"I'm leaning toward the ECBWs myself," Russell continues. "That's what The Science is saying... As long as we get the compliance we need from everyday people, we should be fine. It shouldn't be *too* difficult. I'm not a big eye-looker myself. Not really... The Brits don't tend to be, do they? They tend to be quite reserved."

"That's a good point," says Sean. "Plus with the phones... Are you much of a water-drinker, Mr Drisell?"

Russell Drisell shifts in his seat because he is in pain. Also, because he feels cagey. He's not touched any tap water since he flushed his pot of laughing lotion down the sink and released it out into the world. He's never mentioned what he did, not to a living soul: but gosh how it haunts him. Because, though none of this has been fully joined up in his head, *some part of him saw the lorry bouncing*. He knows something funny/peculiar is afoot, and in his heart of hearts he feels responsible. Long before Barry DeLuxe-Kelson did or didn't empty his truckload of magic into the reservoirs, Russell had convinced himself that he was in some way responsible for bringing civilisation to its brink. And it's why he's dying. That's what he thinks – or feels. Rather, that's the worm that's eating at his insides, stealing his life away.

He adds: "I must admit I'm not much of a water-drinker, no. I don't like the taste. I'm not a big fan of the fizzy drinks either – so it's quite a job to stay hydrated. But I do love tea. And coffee. I love a coffee. Then again, I try to keep the coffee to a minimum, because it tends to keep me awake… and unfortunately I find that's the case with the decaf variety, also…" He shrugs, makes a sort of *whadderyaknow?* sucking noise with his teeth, grinds to an aimless halt.

And there's silence, while they sip. The one who isn't Sean comes to the point.

"We're actually looking for Ozias Plume… There's a warrant on him, *finally*. The powers-that-be have taken their heads out of their you-know-whats and issued an arrest warrant, I'm pleased to say."

Russell nods dully. "That's good," he says.

"Because he has to be stopped. He's doing his uttermost to bring civilisation to the brink. At this point, we just need to get him out of circulation."

"It may be too late," Russell says.

"It may be," agrees Sean. "Nevertheless. Better late than never. We don't know what he might be planning for us next. What sort of further mayhem he has up his sleeve. At least if he's behind bars we can put a stop to that."

"Good point," says Russell. He blows on his tea. Will he be around to see it, the further mayhem Ozias may have up his sleeve? Probably not. Another stab of multi-dimensional fear, and pain, and sorrow.

"… So…" Sean's partner picks up the trail. "We've got officers out searching for him all over the place, and I tell you what," he says, "For such a well-known and recognisable character he's doing a great job of staying out the way. We can't find him. No one can… We thought maybe – it's a long shot – but we thought maybe you might have been in contact with Ms Malone? We think they're probably together… Apologies for any insensitivity… but the situation is… It's dire, Mr Drisell. I don't need to tell you."

Russell says: "This situation has nothing to do with Debs. You realise that, don't you? He's got some terrible hold on her. I'm not giving you information to harm Debs." The words have burst out of him. He didn't realise he was going to say them. Suddenly, he is aware that there are tears in his eyes and a lump in his throat. Worse, he's weeping. He's *weeping.* This is the most humiliating moment of his life.

Sean gets up from the sofa. He crosses the room and pats Russell's heaving shoulder. He is very embarrassed. He looks at his partner, who shrugs, horrified.

There is a long silence. Really – the only sound is Russell, crying. And then either Sean, or the other one, assures Russell that no harm will come to Debs, none whatsoever. They have no idea if this is the truth. But they are out of their comfort zones. Absolutely adrift. Civilisation is on the brink, and in front of them, a man in ski goggles who'd seemed quite sensible only seconds previously, is sobbing uncontrollably.

Russell tells them eventually - partly because he hates Ozias Plume for stealing Debs from him, not that she was ever his; partly because he believes in the system of shared values, and he wants to help put it back together again. He wants to undo some of the damage he feels he has wreaked on the world.

So he tells them about the campervan. He suspects that it's where they're hiding. It's a very nice campervan, he says. He and Debs used it once, to drive all the way across France. It was *the best holiday*, he tells them and almost starts crying again. He says he has the numberplate on a parking app.

So simple.

That's how the police track down Ozias Plume. Because of Russell Drisell's parking app, and because UK is blessed with seven million or so CCTV cameras, many of them working: it's hard for a man in a campervan to go unnoticed.

THE CAMPERVAN

Not that he has ever been in hiding. Or not quite. People in search of his magic seem to know where to find him. When the police officers roll up, there is a crowd of laughing elves standing around the van. (The elves are human size because they are human and not really elves at all, but reminiscent of elves due to their good cheer, sense of purpose and remarkable efficiency of movement.)

Another thing about the elves: they have come in cars, which are parked close by, with their boots wide open; or they have come with rucksacks which are parked at their human-sized feet. One of them, in their enthusiasm, has come on a horse.

In the middle of the melee is a small mountain of open boxes, and inside the boxes, tens of thousands of small sachets of laughing cream. The sachets are being dispersed.

Imagine it, then: a green field with sheep grazing, and a group of forty or so self-identifying elves, loading sachets of magic into various receptacles… movement and purpose, efficiency and joy… It's a busy scene, and to the elves, it is funny. Everything is funny. So they're laughing as they work. And then a police car rolls up. They watch it approach. One of the officers stops to open the gate that separates the field from the road. He closes the gate behind him, climbs back into the car, and the car proceeds in an orderly fashion. It's only a hundred yards between the melee and the gate, and the self-identifying elves find it unaccountably funny to see a police car approaching them so politely. By the time the police officers come to a halt, roll down the windows, there isn't an elf among them not bent double with the joke.

The police officers are being good bunnies, as per government edict, and they are wearing their sunnies. But laughter is infectious. They are smiling as they step out of their vehicle.

"Mr Plume?" says one of them, to one of the elves: he is by far the most recognisable elf among them. Both police officers are staring at him, a little starstruck, due to his great fame.

Everybody laughs. "That's him!" they say. "Have you come to arrest him?"

"Unfortunately, that is correct."

HA HA HA HA HA!

Even Debs can't stop herself from laughing. It will be OK. Everyone knows it's going to be OK. That's why it's so funny.

They put handcuffs on him. They put a bag over his face – apologising as they do so. "For the photo," they say. "They'll want something for the papers. If we put the sunnies on you, you'll probably knock them off, knowing you."

Ozias says (from beneath the sack): "… but I might *not* knock them off…"

He's laughing. Everyone is laughing.

They take a selfie: the good bunnies in their sunnies and the bad bunny in handcuffs, with a sack over his head.

"I'll post that over then," says Det. Inspector Frederic Grover. "That'll put people's minds at rest…"

He sends the image to the office-bods back the station, with a nice caption: Got Him!

But then it's pointed out by his partner, by Ozias, by Debs and by all the other laughing elves, that there's no proof the head in the sack belongs to Ozias Plume. It could belong to anyone.

"Yeah. But we can't show his eyes, can we?" says Det Insp Grover. "People will panic."

The elves drop a few sachets of magic into the police car's open windows.

"Oh, very funny," says Det. Insp. Grover, sarcastically. He thinks he keeps the thrill out of his voice. But they all hear it, due to being so empathetic, so alive, and so intuitive these days.

More laughter.

More and more laughter.

The elves slip some more sachets into the police officers' pockets and the police officers pretend not to feel it.

More and more and more laughter.

It's quite a struggle, getting Ozias into the back of the car.

Debs gives him a hug. It's all going to be OK. That much is obvious by now. Even so, she doesn't like to see him leave – not like this, bundled into a police car with a sack on his head.

They tell each other not to worry, as if 'worry' was a part of their emotional repertoire anymore. But even for the early-version elves like Ozias and Debs, a few conversational ticks remain.

Watching the car roll away, Debs considers how best to use the time.

She will call on Russell. That's how. Whether Russell wants to see her or not. He can't avoid her for ever. She has a key to Plumtree Court – she will let herself into the flat, and she will try her best not to frighten him, and she will try her best to make him feel better.

PLUMTREE COURT AGAIN

It's only a couple of hours since he waved goodbye to his last visitors, the serious policemen. He's been lying in bed, hooked up to his news feed, waiting for the bulletin about Plume's arrest. And there it is! Plume with a sack on his head – Russell has no doubt it's Ozias. The good bunnies have told him so. They have even released a pic of a man with a sack on his head.

There's a flicker of discomfort. The sack on the head seems a bit – as Russell might put it: *OTT.* A little bit dehumanising. On the other hand, Ozias Plume has brought civilisation to its brink. The flicker of dismay is quickly crushed – so quickly that Russell barely registers it at all. Ozias deserves whatever he gets. What Russell feels when he looks at the picture, having denied the initial revulsion, is a warm swelling inside his rotting intestine and broken heart: a sunburst of pleasure at the other man's pain.

Ozias has been humiliated. He has been driven away in handcuffs with a sack on his head. And Russell –

… has played a part in hauling civilisation back from The Brink!

Russell has done that. He did it.

There's an image on the news feed of Debs with her arms around Ozias' neck. Russell can't see her face. But he can recognise her arms, the back of her head. He can recognise her anywhere.

Awwww diddums, she can't be with her precious Ozias now, thinks Russell. *Maybe she'll come back to me. And then I'll tell her where to go. I'll pick her up and throw her out the window. Smash open the window with a hammer and throw her out.*

The sunburst rises to the back of his throat, and he realises he's going to vomit.

He lies back on the pillow, and the tears roll down his cheeks, and he holds onto his belly, which is causing him so much pain. He needs some water. He's thirsty.

He's never felt so thirsty.

He wants a long, cool glass of water. Sip-Safe. Weren't they going to roll out the Sip-Safe by now? The good bunnies? What were they saying about safe water? God, he wants water. He wants to vomit. He wants everything to be the way it was, only he can't remember- how was it, the way he wants it to be? What was it like when it was the way it was when he wanted it to be like that, and the way it will be again, now that he's brought civilisation back from the brink?

Ozias with a sack on his head.

Debs with her arms around his neck.

He clasps his belly, he groans in pain, and then the groaning is too much for him. Everything is too much for him. He opens his mouth, his stomach heaves: his cheek, his lower nostril, his chin are soaked in his own vomit, and he cannot find the will to find a way out. He cannot move.

The door opens. He hears it but can't see it. He is lying on his side, facing the window opposite. But the door opens, and it stays open, and there follows a noisy silence. He knows someone is there, standing there, staring at him. And he is conscious of their dismay - their disgust - at the sight of him, the state of the room, the smell of the sick. He doesn't care. It's probably Death, he thinks. A black-hooded figure with no face and a massive sickle. Death is probably standing at the fire-retardant door, looking at him, thinking: *can I even be bothered to bring this one in?*

Russell laughs, from his puddle of vomit. A splatter of sick hits his chin.

He knows it's Debs. Who else could it be? He doesn't turn to look at her. He just lies there with his back to her and his heart aglow. He says, with a smile:

"I thought you were Death, Debs."

Debs laughs. "Maybe I am. Maybe I've come to put you out of your misery. Looks like I'd be doing you a favour, Russ. What the hell's happened around here?" She steps further into the room. She walks around the side of the bed – their bed, a lifetime ago. It's a tiny room. There's barely space to move at the best of times. This afternoon the floor is littered with rubbish: coke tins and uneaten sandwiches, crisp packets, underwear and cold cups of tea. The ski goggles lie forgotten on the sick-stained pillow by his head.

Debs picks her way through the mess to the small, plastic window beyond the bed. She opens it as far it goes (15cm) and sits down on the edge of the bed so that Russell is facing her. He doesn't move, not even his eyes. He stares at the wall beneath the window. Finally, he says:

"Where are your sunnies, Debs?"

Debs doesn't reply. She puts a hand on his forehead.

"Are you smearing me with your magic lotion, Debs?" he says. He's smiling.

Humour, *again*.

Debs says: "I would dearly love to do that, Russ. But maybe…"

Russell's eyes have closed. He's still clasping his belly. He says: "I think I'm dying Debs. I'm sure of it. It's a very definite feeling I've got. I don't know if other people get it, but I've got it. I know."

"No you're not!" she says. "Of course you aren't!"

Then again, maybe he is.

She's bent over the bed and she's holding him in her arms. "Why would you be dying, Russ? You're still young!"

He says: "Some people die young though don't

they?… Who'd've thought I'd be one of them though? A boring sod like me!"

Debs laughs. "You're not boring, Russ… I mean – you are. We're as boring as each other. You're boring, I'm boring. When you think about it, in a way, *everyone's* boring."

He laughs – again. "You're jabbering, Debs."

"Either that or we're *not* boring… It's a question of perspective."

"I've always been boring," he says. "And yet somehow, you agreed to be my girlfriend. Wonders never cease…"

"We had some good times, Russell. We did."

Russell takes a moment to respond to this. He realises, quite clearly, that no, this is not the case. He says: "I don't think so, Debs. It was always a bit uncomfortable. We were selfish. Both of us tried too hard. Or we didn't try hard enough. Plus we didn't have anything in common…" He laughs, a long, slow laugh: a bit rueful. "Not a single thing, really… I love you, though," he adds. "That is – I love you *now*. Thank you for coming to see me." And each word, as it emerges from his mouth, astonishes him.

"I was wondering," he says after a while, "Would you very much mind taking me to the hospital?"

Debs says: "Of course I can!"

"Thank you," Russell replies.

There's a silence while Russell thinks about how to muster the strength to get out of the bed and Debs thinks about what Russell has said, and how it turns out she loves him after all. "I love you by the way," she says. "I do. *Now.* Very much. And I'm sorry for the pain you're in, and I'm sorry for all the pain I've brought you. I'm sorry."

Russell nods. He looks at her at last, and he smiles. It's a beautiful smile and it lights up his grey face. He makes a little effort and lifts his head off the pillow but then the effort is too great after all. He lets his head fall back again. "Perhaps we should get a taxi to the hospital, do you think? Not sure I'm up to the bus, Debs."

Debs tells him she has the campervan.

And he says, "Oh!"

He's forgotten about all that. "I'm sorry… I shouldn't've told them about it… I was being…" he pauses. Various adjectives suggest themselves: vindictive, cowardly, delusional. He snorts, and mumbles, "silly".

Debs waves it aside. "Come on, then. Let's get going shall we?"

Gently, she sits him up.

He perches on the edge of the bed, looking at his knees, taking a while to gather his strength. He wonders if he will ever return to this flat, this little room: probably not. He ponders the long journey ahead. *God only knows where that'll end*, he thinks.

And he laughs. He feels lightheaded; if not springy of foot, then most definitely springy of spirit. It occurs to him that something is missing. Something feels better than usual.

"Would you mind calling Mum. And Holly... And the guys at work?"

"Of course I can."

"Tell them I love them." He chuckles. They might be shocked to hear it. "… And tell them I'm sorry I was so boring."

Debs nods. She stands up. "You stink of sick, Russ. What do you think about taking a shower?"

So, they teeter to the little bathroom room together, laughing about the coke tins and abandoned underpants, the goggles and the ski holiday they never took. Also, Debs is crying. Maybe they both are. And yet, in its own way, it's a happy occasion: perhaps their happiest together.

The *NEWSPAPER* OFFICES

Eric Leider, editor of Britain's oldest and most respected, possibly the most famous newspaper on the planet, is hiding inside his glass-walled office with the blinds pulled down. He's on the phone to The Newspaper's chairman and he has been on the phone to him for some time. Outside, in the newsroom, there is a growing but unspoken sense of dread that their editor may perhaps have been lost to the other side.

Before the call with the chairman, Mr Leider was on a call to Downing Street.

And that call, the contents of which he is still keeping to himself, also lasted for some time: far longer than usual. On other days, when Downing Street or the chairman 'reach out' to Eric Leider, he takes the call, takes his orders, and hangs up. It's all fairly curt and distasteful. He likes to imagine that these calls don't, ultimately, have any editorial impact; or, better yet, that they don't really happen at all.

However - today - *something funny is up.*

For example: when the PM called, Leider told his secretary to tell the PM he was 'on the pisser', and that he'd call him back 'subito'.

This is not like Leider, whose canny tread, over a thirty-year career, has never been anything but light and tactful and pleasing.

But he strode off to the pisser cackling, leaving his secretary to translate the message as best she could. She said:

"He's temporarily indisposed due to an emergency, Sir. Many apologies, Sir. He will return the call momentarily."

This bought Leider a momentarily or two, but no more than that. When he returned from the pisser, he didn't bother to ring the Prime Minister back.

The PM had to 'reach out' three more times before Leider agreed –was forced – to take the call.

"Tell him I've got an upset tummy," the editor whispered to his secretary, giggling into his intercom, steaming up his sunnies. "Tell him I've got the squittoes!"

Eventually the secretary called the PM direct on her mobile phone, and then she carried her mobile into the editor's office, with the PM on the line.

"Prime Minister? I have Mr Leider right here. He's right here for you, Sir!" she said, and handed the phone to the boss

The editor shook his head frantically, but the secretary only shook her head back. She laid the phone on the desk in front of him and closed his office door behind her. That was half an hour ago.

Since then, she's put not one but *two* calls through from the chairman.

It's possible the chairman and the PM have already spoken with each other this morning. That's what the secretary thinks.

In any case, as previously noted, something funny is afoot.

In the newsroom, behind sunnies and screens and defensive walls of bottled water, those few reporters who have braved the journey into work wait impatiently to be told what stories they may run with. There's not much of the day left. It's getting to the time when it'll be too late to put anything on the pages at all.

In the meantime, for the most part, reporters and staff are at least keeping themselves busy. For example, Kitty Manage, who feels that her important article yesterday – indeed, her bold reporting generally vis a vis the current crisis - might well prove to be a career game-changer, is putting the finishing touches to a massive piece about the medical benefits of sunglasses. At this instant she's pausing in her work to have a chat with Oliver Greengrass, who reports on consumer affairs, because he has an array of twenty or so sunglasses on his desk (he's writing a Best Shades guide), one of which comes with a £3,995 price tag.

"Amazing," Kitty Manage is saying. "They are *stunning* though, aren't they?" She doesn't ask to try them on. Despite writing so authoritatively on the subject, she's uncertain if wearing sunglasses that are only borrowed might interfere with their Eye Contact Beam Wave inhibiting properties, and she prefers to be safe than sorry.

As things stand, tomorrow's newspaper of record, the oldest and most respected, possibly the most famous newspaper in the world, has been laid out as a morale-boosting Sunnies'n'Bunnies summer special. Articles covering every aspect of the sunnie/bunny situation await the editor's green light: *style* and sunnies, *etiquette* and bunnies, Eye Contact Beam Waves and sunny bunnies, *recyclable* sunnies, *famous* bunnies wearing *silly* sunnies, sunnies for business bunnies, sunnies for sporty bunnies, and, of course, sunnies for anxious bunnies who are visually and/or spatially challenged. The team has really gone to town. They've surpassed themselves. David Balls [News Editor] and Sally Lumber [Arts'n'Features] are impressed. They've sent internal messages to all the editorial staff, in and outside of the building, congratulating them on their metal and drive. This is uncharacteristically pleasant of both. But tough situations call for real leadership. David and Sally feel they have risen to occasion.

And then the message comes through from the editor's office: the message they have all been waiting for. His office door is now locked, and the blinds are still down. He's in there talking to someone, possibly himself. His secretary says she hopes it might be the chairman, but she can't be sure. In any case the message from the editor's office is-

That *all* pages for tomorrow's paper can now be sent [to print], except for the front page.

This is not unusual. The front page is often the last to go. Nevertheless--

It would be fucking nice, David Balls believes, *if the fucking editor gave him one fucking clue what the fucking headline was going to be. Not to mention the fucking story. If he even knew what the fucking story was…*

And so on.

There follows a flurry of activity in the mostly empty newsroom. It's not noisy, like it was in the olden days, when David Balls was a cub reporter and cared about the work he did. Today, the flurry involves an uptick in keyboard taps–

And then, cutting through the uptick of taps, muffled behind the glass walls and the locked door and the closed blinds: the sound of the Eric Leider's laughter. Hyena like.

What the fuck is wrong with him, thinks David Balls.

An angry reaction. A ludicrously angry reaction.

More to the point, what the fuck is wrong with David Balls?

A gust of stale air bursts from his tar-clogged lungs. His cheeks twitch. His lips relax.

His shoulders hunch.

His stomach spasms.

He feels better than has in years.

Oops.

ACCIDENT & EMERGENCY ROOM
READING

There's a youngish nurse/receptionist standing behind a glass screen and she looks quite pleased to see them.

"Hello!" says the nurse/receptionist, smiling as they approach.

Russell has his arm around Deb's shoulder, for support. They stagger slowly across the waiting room.

Russell lets go of Debs' shoulder and leans on the counter to catch his breath. The nurse/receptionist says: "You sit down. I'll take your details from your friend, and then we'll get you some wheels. We'll get you some help right away…"

He gives a little groan - a sort of grunt of appreciation, and the nurse laughs. She rolls on her heels and throws back her head.

"I must say," she says, "You look terrible!"

Russell laughs, Debs laughs. "I must say I feel pretty terrible," he replies.

The nurse says: "Well, worry not! You've come to the right place! Help is at hand!"

As Russell settles on the nearest seat he notices there's no one else in the waiting room. No one at all. "Where is everyone?" he asks.

"Good point," says Debs, looking around at the empty room. "These places are meant to be heaving."

The nurse looks at Debs. She looks at Russell. Big, clear eyes. (No sunnies). Beautiful, shiny skin. She says: "I have my own theories. I'm not supposed to share them. Do you want to know what they are?"

Russell and Debs agree that yes, they do.

"Well – we're not getting the drunks, because the urge to get blind drunk tends to fade, doesn't it. We're not getting the fights… same reasoning. So, we're already cutting out a good 70 per cent of the usual traffic. We're not getting the carelessness that leads to the accidents – because people tend to focus, don't they. We're not getting the time wasters – and by the way that's including the staff!" Another big laugh from the receptionist/nurse. "Trust me, we're the biggest time wasters of all! And that leaves – well, right now that leaves you, right? Ok… Let's get you checked in..."

She glances at Russell, whose skin is shiny and who is chuckling again, for no obvious reason. But there's a light in his eyes which has turned inward, and it seems to the nurse, who has seen this light many times before, that there's not much to be done for him now, and that he knows this better than any of them. The nurse slides paperwork and a pen across the counter towards Debs. She unlocks the partition door between reception desk and waiting room and goes to sit in the chair beside Russell.

She says: "Are you in a lot of pain? It seems like maybe you may be."

"Ha!" says Russell. "Maybe I may be!" He likes that. "May-*be* I may-*be*! Nice!…" And then, more solemnly, "I must admit, I am. In quite a lot of pain." The nurse rests a hand on the back of his. It's nothing much, but then again, it's enough. Being so intuitive now, Russell feels the empathy, absorbs the kindness. "Thank you," he says.

"'Thank you'?" she says, looking at him with her big, clear eyes. "What for?" She stands up. "Wait there. I'm going to get you some wheels."

There's no waiting. The nurse and Debs wheel Russell into the inner sanctum, where the doctors are, and the comfortable beds, and also, Russell hopes, some good, strong painkillers.

Two doctors tend to him, not just one. They shine a torch into the eyes where the light has turned inward. They ask him questions, slide him under machines, prod him, ask him a hundred more questions, some of them quite stupid – stupid enough to make everyone giggle.

Debs says: "Do you know what's wrong with him?"

Russell laughs sadly.

Debs says: "Is it too late?"

And Russell laughs – again.

Debs says: "Fuck's sake, Russell. *Stop laughing!*"

At which point everyone laughs: the nurse, the two doctors, the person with a mop, who is standing around in the background, listening in, Russell – and finally, Debs.

The doctors ask Russell how he wants to deal with the situation, and Russell says: I would like to go back to Plumtree Court. If it's not inconvenient. If you can give me some painkillers, for when it becomes – if it ever becomes, you know, *unbearable*… I've got money now, so I can get Deliveroo. I think that's probably the best option. The least-worst option..."

Debs says: "I'm not leaving you to die all alone in that soulless flat, Russell. I'm definitely not going to do that."

"But I love it there," he says. "When we left I wasn't even sure I'd ever make it back. Now that I know I can, I feel quite cheerful… well… maybe cheerful's a bit strong…"

"You could come and live with us in the campervan, Russell, if you like?" says Debs. "Or we could get you one of your own, and you could just be next door to us, in your own campervan if you prefer, and I can look out for you. How about that? That might work. Please don't go back to that horrible flat."

Russell says: "I don't think it's horrible, Debs. I think it's comfortable and modern and… and… sophisticated. I think it's the most comfortable and sophisticated place I've ever lived.' He laughs. "Debs, I love that horrible flat. I actually think it's beautiful!"

Debs stares. They all stare. Russell's shiny face

is gaining a little colour.

"I love the tarmac in the garden," he continues, "because it's tidy. I love the twenty-four hour lighting, because, to me, it says Welcome Home… I love the windows that don't open, and the fire doors that slam shut, and the posters in the corridors telling me to hold onto the handrail because *to me* all that stuff is proof that people care about each other. *To me,* it says the Plumtree Managing Board actually cares that we don't get injured…"

A moment passes. Everyone tries quite hard not to laugh.

They fail. Russell doesn't mind. He knows it's ridiculous. He knows he's ridiculous, and he doesn't care *one tiny bit*. He loves his flat. So he laughs along with them, and he continues regardless. "I love the telly above the bath, Debs… even though it's broken. I love that we lived there together once, albeit not very happily. *I love that soulless flat*. It's my home. There's nowhere else I want to be."

Silence in the courtyard, silence in the street.

No one is laughing any more. Russell means what he says. They nod, trying to understand.

"It sounds like a lovely flat," the nurse says eventually. "A telly above the bath?"

"Yes, but it's broken," Russell reminds her.

"Even so… Well… Anyway…" she looks

embarrassed. An idea has occurred to her.

It's also occurred to the doctor on her left, who knows the ins and outs of the nurse's private life, which is a mess at the moment. The nurse has a little boy, aged three.

"Haven't you just broken up with your fella?" that doctor says. "Where are you living at the moment?"

"Ah!" says the nurse.

Doctors, Nurse/Receptionist, Debs and Russell, being all very intuitive these days, see the solution at once. Russell doesn't want to live out his final days in a campervan with Ozias and Debs. Actually, he doesn't want to live out his final days with Debs, not anymore. His father is dead, his mother is in a care home, and his sister Holly has her hands full with the children… Meanwhile the Nurse/Receptionist and her young son urgently need a place to live. Problems solved. Most unexpectedly.

The nurse worries that her little boy might be a bit much for a dying man. Russell worries that a dying man might be a bit much for the little boy. The doctors are certain that both Russell and the nurse are worrying unnecessarily. The boy is so young he won't, with luck, have much of a clue what's going on, and there's no doubt in anyone's mind that his presence will cheer everyone up.

Debs gets quite bossy. She's going to use the campervan to help the nurse move her stuff. She says the nurse and the little boy should take the bedroom, and that Russell should move into the little study.

"I'll try to stay out of the way," Russell says.

"So shall we," says the nurse. "But this is perfect. Isn't it? You won't be alone at night, which is the main thing; and we'll have a roof and a bed, and we'll both have little Hennrick to keep us on our toes!"

56

Sensible Su's rich husband needs to get his money out of reach and himself out the UK as fast as possible, before he catches this appalling disease and starts giving everything away.

The newspapers drone on about waxy skin and inappropriate laughter. It's the impulsive, irresponsible, ill-conceived 'generosity' that terrifies him. The Giving Mania, as his rich pals have named it. A very frightening form of insanity. He's aware of several extremely well-off people, former friends, now afflicted, who've been giving things away willy-nilly – literally, houses and cars and millions of pounds, just on the spur of a moment. Just because they felt like it. Sensible Su's rich husband can't stop thinking about this. He's been shuddering all day.

He has insulated himself here at the house. He

has surrounded himself with appropriate PPE: sunglasses, rubber gloves, woolly hats, face masks, plastic wrapping, water bottles, kettles, thermometers, anti-bacterial wipes... He is too afraid to step outside in case the mania strikes, and he finds himself donating things to passers-by.

Torn between claustrophobia and terror, he has spent most of the day trying to get through to the private jet companies, or trying to lock his money into mania-proof trust funds where he won't be able to reach it until the storm passes, if it ever does. But it's very difficult to get through to anyone. The banks' websites are down, the trading websites are down; in fact, all financial service websites have been down all afternoon, and nobody's answering their sodding phones.

He has a ferocious headache, and he is livid. Livid with the private jet companies who won't shunt him to the front of the line, livid with the idiocy of people careless enough to catch this appalling disease, livid with Ozias Plume for championing it, livid with God for inventing it, and above all, livid with his wife. She's been sitting on her so-called Inquiry all week. She should have seen this coming.

To be fair, which he is not, she tried to call him a few times yesterday. As usual, he didn't pick up. As usual, he texted her:

"Is it urgent?"

To which she had replied, "Not really! ☺"

And so, he'd left it.

As it happens he hasn't laid eyes on her since yesterday. He was out last night, and they sleep in separate bedrooms. He tends to tiptoe into and out of the house to avoid having to deal with her, or speak to her, or even to hear her voice, which is soft and low, but which grates on him nonetheless. (She's nervous around him. She sucks up. It only makes it worse.) If he weren't so keen on his money, he might have divorced her years ago.

Yesterday she went AWOL, not that he noticed. After they bundled her out of the boring room and fired her from the panel – something he's not yet been made aware of – she wandered the London streets, making new friends and giggling at all the new things that were funny. She came home with a sachet of laughing lotion, given to her by a man in a pub who assured her he had more than enough and that anyway, there wasn't much need for it anymore, since everyone seemed to be catching the vibe (as he confusingly referred to it) with or without the lotion making direct contact with the skin.

And then he started singing to her the Bob Dylan song Ozias Plume had been singing earlier. The whole pub joined in, including Su.

The answer, my friend…
Is blowing in the wind…
The answer is blowing in the wind!

Su could not contain her delight.

"A pub sing-along!" she said, over and over again. "I didn't think they existed except in films about Irish people!"

She left the pub with the sachet, and a mission, and the Bob Dylan song stuck in her head.

That was yesterday. Today, this afternoon, Su's husband is so exhausted by rage and fear that he has collapsed onto the sofa in his luxurious kitchen, and is lying there, flat out, surrounded by the detritus of his paranoia (aforementioned), and with both shoes on the cushions. He is holding his aching head, fixating on the horrors of his possible poverty, while simultaneously wondering if there's anyone in the vicinity who might make him a cup of tea. He shouts for the housekeeper, but then he remembers she's just put her head round the door and told him she was taking the dog for a walk.

She should have waited until he knew he wanted tea.

'Su?' he bellows. '… Su?… SU!' … He's actually about to stand up: do battle with the abdominal muscles and the balance and the outsize belly and so on - but then Su hears him shouting and she comes scurrying.

"Oh," he says, "you're here." He glances at her, in preparation for feeling irritated. She's beaming at him. He glances again. Frowns. "You look different," he says.

Su has a plan. She's put powder on her face to dull the shininess, just in case. She has the sachet in her hand, and her hand behind her back.

"Do I?" she says.

"You look happy."

"I always look happy!" she says.

Typical, he thinks. *Stupid* and *irritating*. Also, not true. "No you don't," he snaps, and then – an unusual turn of events – he continues to look at her. Not only that, he smiles.

Something about her reminds him of when he used to love her, years ago. And for a moment he forgets about the money that's in danger of pouring itself down the drain. He forgets to find her irritating. He just feels sad. He says: "Could you make me a cup of tea?" And as he says it, he realises he's ashamed.

A pinprick of light.

The question pops madly into his head: *why can't you make your own cup of tea?*

He doesn't have an answer. It's just the way it is and always has been. If the housekeeper is walking the dog, Su makes the tea.

Su is still smiling. Now, she starts to laugh. She stands there, giggling, for ages.

He stares at her. "What's wrong with you?" he asks.

"Nothing!" she gasps, clutching her belly with the free hand. "Nothing at all… But I don't know why you can't make your own cup of tea... The kettle's only over there!"

He does not know what to say. Beneath their puffy lids, the eyes bulge. How dare she? *How dare she?*

She sees this. Being so empathetic these days, she feels his rage, and beneath that, his confusion and fear. It's pathetic. *He* is pathetic: he has allowed himself to become pathetic. She sees this now, quite clearly. It's funny and it's tragic. It's comi-trag. Or tragi-com? Either way, she can't stop laughing. Yet still, she finds she loves him. She waves the free hand, body shaking with laughter. She says: "Don't worry, my darling. I'll do it. I'll make you some tea. You wait there!"

He says, with as much dignity as he can muster: "Thank you, Susan."

And off she trots, giggling, filling the kettle, emptying the sachet into cup. Licking her fingers – *yum*! – asking him if he wants biscuits.

*

Sensible Su's rich husband feels like he's having a heart attack as the magic permeates. There was a chink of light. A pinprick of light.

The answer, my friend–
... can lie in the smallest of pinpricks.

For a man like Su's husband, corrupt, greedy, proud, disagreeable – the magic has to really *burrow* to find its way in.

The *NEWSPAPER* OFFICES

Snorting sounds from the inner sanctum. Eric Leider's secretary has knocked on his office door four or five times, to no avail. She can hear him mumbling, and then laughing, mumbling and laughing, and smacking the table, and typing and snorting… It is highly mysterious.

She has an ear to the glass wall. He seems to be banging a rhythm on the desk. And that's all very well, but she's due to go home quite soon, and they still don't have a front page.

"Mr Leider?… Mr Leider, are you ok?"

Nothing.

And then:

"Duh-da-da-daaa--
Duh da-da-dahhh…"

Sensing a crisis, Kitty Manage has come to join her. Kitty has stepped up to a leadership role. "Someone has to," she says to the secretary, who is quite close to tears. Sally Lumbar

(Arts'n'Features), having sent off all her pages, has already scurried home, with no intention of returning, ever again. David Balls (News) ought to be standing where Kitty stands now. He ought to be the one banging on Eric Leider's door, but he's currently bent over his computer, face hidden, pretending he hasn't noticed what's going on.

Kitty and the secretary look at each other. It is time for action.

Kitty says: "Get Maintenance up here, Sophie. We're going to have to force the door."

"Really?" says Sophie (the secretary). "But we can hear him in there. He hasn't fainted or anything."

Kitty says it again, more forcefully this time. "It's not the point. We don't know what he's doing in there. *All we know for sure is that he's laughing…*"

A solemn moment between the two women. Kitty has made a good point.

So, the secretary nods. She dials Maintenance. Maintenance doesn't pick up.

"Duh-da-da-da-derr –
Duh-dada daahh-daahh."

"… Oh God…" moans the secretary. "What's he's doing in there?"

From the other side of the door comes a big belt of laughter, the noisiest yet. And then some keyboard hammering.

Kitty bangs on the door. "Eric? We really need-David says we really need the front page… Are you in here?"

A pause.

A crash. Eric Leider shouts: "SEND!" And they hear him laughing - *again*: a bellow of shameless laughter. To the women outside he sounds demented.

"Do you think he's got the bug?" whispers the secretary.

Duhhhh (da-da)

Kitty Manage shakes her head. "Of course not," she says quickly. Her mind is boggling. Not Eric. Not Eric Leider. Not the editor! "… It's just not possible," she adds.

The women hear him pushing back his chair. They leap away, pretend to be in conversation with one another.

And then the door springs open and out he bounds.

Everything about him is awry. His sunglasses are falling off, his shirt is untucked, he's taken his shoes off. His thick dark hair, normally kept in order with expensive oils, is pinging out in corkscrew curls all over his head.

"GUYS!" he shouts. "GUYS-GUYS-GUYS! I've had a brainwave! Everyone! Come over here!"

There are fifteen or so people still lingering in the room. They shuffle up, surly, suspicious, a little fearful. They wait.

He's grinning at them, one by one. He wants to say something, but he keeps laughing. He's rubbing his hands together, then holding a finger up as if about to speak and then folding over into helpless laughter yet again.

"Where's Balls?" he says at last. "Don't tell me Balls has gone home?"

David Balls is still at his computer, hiding his face. He can't speak, because he, too, is laughing uncontrollably. From behind the computer, he raises a hand in the air.

"Over here," Balls mutters. "Just… doing something…"

The editor clocks this. Being so intuitive suddenly, he clocks an ally. He says it again:

"GUYS I'VE HAD A BRAINWAVE!"

The guys look limp and blank and irritable. They wait.

Eric Leider looks at them again, one by one. He's smiling so broadly there is a spillage of dribble on his chin. He cannot stop. He simply cannot stop smiling. Why didn't he think of this brainwave years ago?

He says: "Let's–" He pauses. "Instead of–" He pauses again. He beams at the journalists. "Guys, seriously, let's *find stuff out and then report on it!*"

He looks around the room.

Nothing.

Silence.

Limp. Blank. Irritable. One hundred per cent confusion.

Kitty Manage speaks for them all when she says, quite angrily: "With all due respect Eric, as *Newspaper* journalists that's what we're trained to do, and I think you will find it's what we've all been doing for some time. We investigate. We report. We speak truth to power."

Guffaws from David Balls at the back. They turn to look at him – everyone turns, that is, except for Eric Leider, who is bent double, creased up with his own laughter.

The journalists look at each other. They look at Eric Leider, and they look at David Balls, who has never revealed the slightest hint of humour about anything, ever, until this moment. Realisation dawns.

Their editors have fallen.

They are on their own. And they are terrified.

Kitty Manage is also terrified but – to her credit - unlike the others, she doesn't immediately scurry for her coat. Kitty believes in The *Newspaper*. Something like that. She believes that she believes what she says she believes. So – she digs in:

"But have we got a splash? This is ridiculous, Eric. *What are we putting on the front page?* We need to send the front page, and we need to send it *NOW*."

Eric Leider's knees buckle. He is laughing with such relish, such magical abandon, that his legs can no longer support his weight. He rolls onto the floor, holding his belly, gasping for breath. Tears are pouring down his face.

Laughter is infectious. From their desks, as they collect their stuff and prepare to scram, one or two small chuckles escape from the journalists. A few, and then a few more. They're all laughing. Even Kitty Manage can't stop herself from smiling.

With his cheek on the carpet, his knees pulled up to his chest, the editor finally answers Kitty's question.

"Front page… gone…" he gurgles. "…Already gone… I just sent it... A poem…"

His voice is muffled by the carpet. No one is listening, anyway.

The *NEWSPAPER*

THE SITUATION SO FAR

A POEM BY ERIC LEIDER, 52YRS

Everyone's happy and everything's funny
And nobody cares about power or money
Let's drink-the-drink to Lily the pink–

CIVILISATION IS ON THE BRINK!

DAY SIX

No sign of Lord Stevens of Dirkmass and Stirton, and certainly no sign of Sideline Su. Of the three panellists, only Dame Davina has turned up to work this morning. Beside her, looking even more like an angry pixie than usual, sits her recently anointed *Deputy* panellist, the former Mayor of London, Mr Trunot Salvy.

He always looks quite like a pixie, due to his tiny body, small, bad-tempered facial features and oddly pointy ears. He is looking especially angry and pixie-like at this instant because, until a few moments ago, he had been led to understand that he was joining Dame Davina on the panel of this Ad Hoc Non Statutory Public Inquiry as an equally valid component. She's just now informed him otherwise, and with some sternness, too.

"I would have thought it would have been obvious," she snapped. "But as my Deputy, it's not in your remit to issue statements or edicts without my previous say-so."

Trunot Salvy had been thunderstruck. He asked Dame Davina to clarify, and she had been happy to do so.

"I am the *Lead* panellist, Trunot," she reiterated. "You are the *Deputy*. And as such, all Inquiry-related pronouncements – indeed, all or any statements, guidelines, observations and rulings must be passed through, and announced by, me. There are protocols and I must ask you to observe them."

A few seconds before this (what had solicited Dame Davina's outburst), in reaction to a particularly noisy burst of giggles from the Everyday Benches, Trunot had leaned into the microphone *without so much as a by your leave*, and announced a New Rule for the boring room. The rule was:

Anyone who laughs writes 200 lines during break. (Something like that.)

Dame Davina had been livid.

She still is. Actually, she's been livid since the day before yesterday, and today she's so livid it's making it hard for her to keep the veins from bursting through her face. She can feel them now, throbbing away. And that's even *now*, after the relief afforded to her, putting Trunot Salvy back in his place.

"Lead panellist?" he repeats. "I had understood-"

"Trunot," (she snaps) "As my Deputy in this AdHocNonStatutoryPublicInquiry, it is not for *you* to be making up new rules. As she glares at him her vision swims with rage, and malice, and her neck and face begin to merge. "We are not at City Hall now, my dear!" she says.

The angry pixie considers how best to respond to this. In the meantime, he titters politely. It occurs to him he may have made a dreadful mistake by agreeing to be here today. On the other hand – yesterday, before she called, he was watching Netflix, eating nuts and feeling forgotten. Today he had a limousine come to drive him in to work, just like the good old days. He feels double the man he did yesterday. So.

Be careful what you wish for a little voice says.

He tips his pixie head. "I do apologise," he says to Dame Davina. "I may have jumped the gun."

She tips her balloon head to acknowledge the apology. Yes, indeed he may have done. Apology accepted.

Peace restored. They return their attention to the boring room, and a glum silence falls.

What now?

It's not looking good out there.

Given the headlines – the headline - this morning, it's surprising anyone has turned up at all. What is becoming increasingly obvious to Trunot and Davina, though they haven't yet acknowledged it aloud, is that those who have turned up are not taking the proceedings very seriously. Far from it. They keep mucking about with their sunglasses, putting them on at funny angles and laughing about how silly they look.

Dame Davina breaks the glum silence. She mutters to Trunot, or possibly to herself: *"Right then."*

She switches on her mic and leans in:

"Please be aware that sunnies should be worn according to government guidance. They should be balanced across the *upper* bridge of the nose. Lenses must cover the eyes and must *at all times* remain *parallel* with the ground. Anyone who removes their sunnies, or thinks it's amusing to wear them at a 'funny' angle, will be taken from this room and-"

They're laughing.

They're defying her!

Dear God! They're wobbling their sunnies all over their stupid faces! They're removing their sunnies altogether and–

"… taken from this room and detained in police cells until such a time…"

She has to raise her voice to be heard over their laughter. They're rolling on the benches! They're throwing their sunnies into the aisles!

"… detained in police cells until such a time as I see fit to release them..."

Like heatwaves, the laughter rises off the benches, fuzzing the focus, making nonsense of the room.

"Be aware there is a MAXIMUM PENALTY… A MAXIMUM PENALTY of–"

Boy, is she angry.

"A MAXIMUM PENULTY OF LIFE IMPRISONMENT!"

Trunot Salvy clears his throat. "Are we sure about that?" he whispers.

The blood is pounding so hard in her ears, she can't hear him. "CALL THE FIRST WITNESS!" she yells.

But there are no witnesses today, as she knows well – or did, before she lost her temper. None of them has bothered to turn up. *No one* has turned up to this ludicrous and now, clearly redundant, Ad Hoc Non Statutory Public Inquiry, except for Dame Davina and Trunot Salvy and a bunch of hooligans who've only come here to laugh.

She looks across to the VP Box. Eight people. So called 'journalists'. *And they're all fucking laughing.*

"SILENCE!" she bellows.

"Davina," mutters Trunot. He's growing alarmed. "I think you should maybe calm down!"

She switches off her mic and leans back in her chair. Her eye is caught, once again, by this morning's *The NEWSPAPER*. Trunot brought it in, in case she hadn't seen. The sight of it makes her stomach turn. The sight of it, at this instant, fuels her rage and desperation. Civilisation is on the brink. Her world is on the brink. She says to Trunot:

"We have to lock them in!"

Trunot says: "*Who? Who do we have to lock in?*"

"All of them," Dame Davina replies. "Lock them

all in. And switch off the lights. It'll bring them to their senses."

Trunot hesitates. He looks from Dame Davina, beside him, to the fizzing, fuzzing, not-so-boring room below, and then to the VP Box, which appears to be - *floating*? He rubs his eyes. He didn't sleep well last night. Either way - it's mayhem out there. It's mayhem everywhere. He's read the papers. Rather, he's seen *The NEWSPAPER*. He's looked out of the car window during the limousine drive in. Something clearly needs to be done – but…

"Doesn't sound very legal," he mumbles.

She turns her face to frighten him. And she succeeds. She looks very frightening. She says: "I'll tell you what's legal, Trunot! Lock them in!"

At this point, the former mayor submits. Happily. He is out of his comfort zone, as he will explain later, should anyone ask. He is, after all, only obeying orders. Protocols are there to be observed and he is only the Deputy. He is glad to be led.

*

After a little research, however, it becomes clear - *unfortunately* (he breaks it to her softly) - that what she's demanded of him is impossible. That is, *yes,* they can lock the VPs into the VP Box – what few VPs remain. They can't lock the larger room because it requires keys, pin codes, and the cooperation of security guards, none of whom, with the greatest respect, are willing to help out.

Dame Davina sends Trunot Salvy to wedge a chair against the door to the VP's exit. Off he trots. She is a powerful kind of woman, especially now, when she's scared and angry.

She puts in a call to Lord Stevens. Her thirteenth of the morning, and her thirteenth to be ignored. She knows what he's doing. She knows what he's done, and she's never loathed or despised anyone quite as much as she despises Lord Stevens of Dirkmass and Stirton this morning.

Coward, she thinks. *Traitor*. *Weakling*. Somewhere in the mix, she feels rejected. Bitterly, cruelly, viciously, unforgivably overlooked and left behind. How she hates him, and everyone who has ever made her feel bad. The hatred keeps her busy until Trunot returns.

And when he returns and assures her that the job is done and that the chair is properly wedged, she addresses the everyday people on the Everyday Benches for the last time.

"Go home, plebs," she says. "There will be no public permitted at the Public Inquiry today."

LAW ENFORCEMENT
with
LAUGHNG LOTION

The Global Health people over in Gstaad have not

grounded all flights. Private airplanes, carrying important people in sensible eyewear, are still very much allowed. And there's nothing nature abhors more than a gap in the market.

Fortunately for important people like Chak, a large number of albeit slightly mucky airplanes (previously reserved for ferrying the everydays on their environment-wrecking holidays) have been spruced up and released for sale at lightning speed. And clever Chak has managed to nab one.

He's not the only one. It's mayhem at the airports.

Who knew there were so many important people in sensible eyewear living on the island, and all with enough spare cash to buy themselves a plane?

And how awkward for them – the actors and the singers, the bankers, the politicians, the tv stars, the government and media and corporation and NGO heads… how *awkward* for them that they should find themselves lumped together, so rich, so important, so exposed, and so desperate for a ride - just as this madness is unfurling!

*

In the reception area of a New Forest police station, Ozias Plume and friends are clustered around the front desk, staring at a computer screen.

All but one of the station's cell doors have been opened. The single cell that remains locked contains a man arrested for murder and rape earlier this morning. Everyone (being so intuitive now) recognizes that there is no light in him at the current time. Not even a pinprick. Were he to be released, he would only return to the world to cause more suffering. So, he has to stay where he is. Everyone else is free to go.

And yet they linger, transfixed.

An air traffic professional named Brian Hayse is live feeding the unfurling madness from the control tower at Paragmar Park, Britain's busiest private airport. Today Paragmar Park is busier than busiest. It's busier than it was ever built to be. There are airplanes jostling for space as far as the horizon: beyond the airport's perimeter fences and out onto the motorway. Hundreds of them. And though the feed keeps glitching, because of the volume of people around the world logging in, and though Brian Hayse and colleagues appear to be communicating with the pilots and each other in wholly incomprehensible jargon, everyone, everywhere (being so intuitive these days) feels the same thing, and though they don't really know why, they're already laughing.

Then Debs calls Ozias on his mobile, recently restored to him. She's back at Plumtree Court.

Ozias says: "Debs! Are you watching this?"

And yes, of course she is. She and Russell Drisell, and Grace (the nurse) and her three-year-old son, Hennrick, are watching it on Grace's computer, just now installed. Debs is calling in the hope Ozias might shed some light on the situation, since he often passed through the same airport in his previous life, when he too was an important person.

He can't shed any light. He's as confused as anyone, he replies.

She says: "Have you been released yet? I presume yes, if you're answering your phone. Are you ok?"

Conversational ticks. Of course he's OK.

"I am *well*," he says. "And I'm very happy to hear your voice. Shall I come and join you? Or is that awkward and unkind? How is Russell? How's he feeling?"

"He's very ill," Debs says. "Much iller than any of us realized – except for him. He knew." She glances at Russell. He's on the sofa, looking weak and drawn, but rapt by the Paragmar airport scenes. He's chuckling away. It was his idea to ask Debs to ask Ozias if he could shed any light on what was going on down there. So, he glances up from the live feed and smiles at Debs, and the smile is also intended for Ozias. Debs, being intuitive, picks this up and smiles back at Russell with warmth, and love, and enormous gratitude. "Thank you," she says to him.

Russell says: "Tell him to come over – if he

wants. He can meet Grace and Hennrick. And they can meet him, which would be nice, I think. Also – I mean – he sent me all that money, Debs. I owe him a drink." Russell winks.

Ha.

Quite funny, anyway... Debs knows he's paid off the mortgage on Plumtree Court and has already given most of the remaining money to his sister, Holly, who has small children. She wonders what he's going to do with the rest, now that he's going to die; and Russell laughs, because it's obvious to him what she's thinking. It always was obvious, actually, it occurs to him. It was just that he was frightened of her before.

Grace and Henrick are busy watching the airplanes.

Russell taps his nose and winks - again. He mimes writing things down and sweeping things in their direction. And it's all a bit much for Debs. Tears start rolling. She says to Ozias to come on over, fast as he can, so he can help with moving furniture; and then she hangs up and goes to sit next to Russell on the sofa.

THE JOKE
at
PARAGMAR PARK AIRPORT
(Which was Never Meant to be Unkind)

Lord Stevens of Dirkmass and Stirton, for favours unspecified plus a half million pounds, has cadged a space in an airplane belonging to Sir Nicholas James. He's sitting beside an empty seat which had been reserved for his wife, before he caught her giggling. *Giggling.* When he heard it, his body went cold, and then he did what he had to do - what any right-thinking person would do in the circumstances: he pulled over the car and ordered her out.

"I can't allow it," he said. "I simply can*not*, darling. Much as I would love to bring you along, as you know, it would be grotesquely irresponsible. We have to think of the others. Exposing the others to that sort of risk… The point of the exercise, my darling one, is for those of us who are not infected, to *shield*; not simply for the sake of ourselves, but for the sake of the way of life we hold dear. So that we can be there, ready to restore order when this wretched thing blows over."

"*If* it blows over," giggled the wife.

"Which it will, *rest assured.*"

Lady Stevens collected herself, nodded solemnly and climbed out of the car.

"I want you to stay at home, my poppet. Stay at home and *hold the fort* – all right? Until it all blows over. I'll send you money!"

… But by then he was already winding up the window and pulling away.

Lady Stevens was giggling again, in any case. She was holding - not so much the fort, as the dog, which was mostly what she cared about. She had her suitcase at her feet, and it wasn't too long a walk back to the house. Really, honestly – she was pleased to see the back of him.

So she wasn't with Lord Stevens on the plane. Which was nice because it meant he could stretch out.

Behind him, on this small, privately owned airplane, there are fifteen or so odds and sods, their partners and pets: Ahmet Jackal, the shadow Chancellor of the Exchequer, Sir Ranton Bibs, head of the Civil Service; Francis Brune-Cybile, founder of Starbrok-Unwin Hedge fund; Flavia Gerbals, Head of Raymond Blub Investments, Urwin Gist, CFO for Jinty Pharmaceuticals; Timothy Kent, Foreign Secretary, Alison Trudeau, Oscar winning actress and UN Good Will Ambassador, Alyc Hughs, Producer of the reality TV show 'Strip Holiday'… and so on. Lord Stevens of Dirkmass and Stirton feels he's in good company, befitting to his station. He has his head down and the morning's *The NEWSPAPER* in front of him - as if he were actually reading the tripe on the front page.

Not that anyone would know it from his body language, but he is very, very tense. He's thinking mostly about his wife, the gluten- free Emily (Lady Stevens). Inside his horrible head, the thoughts are sloshing around a bit like this:

An allowance for Emily, obviously. Freeze the cards. Freeze all the cards. Clear out any accounts she can access. Somehow ban her from selling – giving – selling– IS SOMEBODY LAUGHING? Did Ranton Bibs just–? No… Dear God, will this plane ever take off? Emily can't get her hands on the – the – What if it's a trick? What if she wasn't really laughing? What if nobody's *really laughing? What if she was pretending to laugh so could she run off with the money? What if she's already taken it? What if she's-*

And then his phone rings, and it's Dame Davina again –And at least that brings a smile to his lips. She wants to know when he's coming back to the panel. Either that, or she's reading *The NEWSPAPER* front page, just like everyone else, and she wants to cadge a lift. Ha ha ha. *In what world?*

Hallelujah! The plane eases forward. One step… Two step… Three step... Four...

This has happened several times over the past hour or so. Each time, it fills Lord Stevens of Dirkmass and Stirton with a fresh blast of hope. *At bloody last!*

- But then the plane eases backwards again.

Four step… Three step…. Two step…

 One.

The plane stops. Again.

A collective groan fills the cabin.

Sir Nicholas James decides it's time to protest. "I've had enough of this," he says. He's angry. "What the actual fuck is going on?" He's unstrapping himself, standing up to confront the pilot. The plane has been farting around for fucking hours and there's still no indication of when they might be cleared for take-off. It's intolerable, considering the money Nicholas spends at this airport, with this crew, on this plane, etcetera. Also, he isn't stupid. There are planes outside his window, stretching to infinity and beyond. And so far as Nicholas James can see, they're all being led the same chaotic dance:

Roll-two-three–

Back-two-three–

STOP.

Step-*Up* two-three, fucking-*clap* two-three. Fucking *kiss-the*-fucking-BRIDE two-three.

Nicholas James, as shaken by recent developments as any sensible BigWallet would be, is not quite his calm and collected self. He's standing up and he's banging on the pilot's door. He's bawling obscenities at the pilot, spewing his observations re. kissing brides and do-si-dos and the outrage of being fucking *kept waiting* – The plane lurches again, more violently this time:

Shunt-two-three.

And Nicholas James, so good at everything

including fly-fishing – is knocked off his feet. His elegant, athletic body catapults backwards. It splatters onto the central aisle, crashing into people's shins and their newspapers, spilling their peanuts and champagne glasses.

He lies there, immobile, covered in peanuts: too angry to speak.

Luckily, nobody laughs.

There's a beat, while nobody does this.

And then they gasp and cry out, as though, of all the things that have occurred in their worlds this past week, this small tumble is the calamity. As if nothing mattered more to any one of them than the possibility that Sir Nicholas James might have bruised his ankle.

Are you ok? Are you all right? What a fall! Is the pilot drunk? Should we call a doctor? Oh my goodness what a tumble! Nicholas are you all right? ARE YOU OK?

And so on. It does nothing to improve Sir Nicholas's mood. He stands up, brushes off the peanuts. And the plane lurches again. *Back* -two -three.

To-the-*left* two-three

Sweep two-three. PAUSE

The movements are becoming bolder. They are becoming extremely annoying. People's sunnies are getting dislodged, their stuff is sliding onto the floor. Nicholas' passengers fully forget their worries vis a vis their host and his hurty ankle. This is serious.

Out of the window, they see airplanes rolling to the left, rolling to the right…

… And the airplanes are moving… is it possible? *The airplanes are all moving together, in almost perfect union!* A landscape of giant metal dancing machines!

Somewhere in the dancing mix, a few dozen planes to the left, Jacinda Plume is locked in the toilet. She has a copy of the morning's *NEWSPAPER* in one hand, and she's so afraid of catching the ECBWs that she's vomiting into the toilet bowl. There's vomit on her cream-beige trousers. There's vomit on *The NEWSPAPER*. She's retching and puking, and Chak Bruton, whose nostrils are crusty with cocaine, is yelling at her through the toilet door to get back in her seat and to calm *the fuck* down. To the right of Chak's plane, in another plane, the bass guitarist of the world's biggest rock band is holding tight to a man who invented an app for currency exchange. They're both sobbing, and have been for hours, since the moment they left their amazing houses; and beyond them, in another plane, a woman who created bottom-accentuating underpants is cradling a man who invented a weight loss pill that causes strokes in a minority of cases; a dozen planes along from them, various members of the British Royal family are attempting to kick down the pilot's door; and directly behind the Royal plane, a man who made a fortune out of faulty wind turbines crouches in the corner of his private cabin, sucking his two middle fingers.

And still the airplanes dance.

And then, somehow, across the tarmac and onto the motorway, from each and every pilots' cabin, there comes the sound of music. A waltz. A bloody *waltz*. The one they used in the advert for – what was it? Who cares? It's one of the most famous music pieces in the world. Everybody knows it and loves it, except now.

Switch off that fucking music, bawls Sir Nicholas James.

SWITCH OFF THAT FUCKING MUSIC bawl the buffeted dignitaries, one and all.

But nobody attends to them, and the music builds.

And it builds.

It's the *Blue Danube*– maybe? Or no, the *Waltz of the Flowers*? And it's beautiful, even through the airplane speakers; and it's light, and it's gathering momentum, and it's playing in time with the dips and sways of all the little airplanes. And the louder it plays, the more graceful and energetic the dancing grows, and the more the dignitaries bawl.

Inside the cabins: champagne, sunnies and peanuts fly. People scream.

And outside: a giant, tarmac ballroom: The Waltz of the Little Airplanes.

In his control tower, air traffic professional Brian Hayse can only record what happens on the tarmac. But he has the waltz music overlayed on the live feed. He's shaking with laughter. Everyone in the control room is shaking with laughter: and yet, their focus remains. The focus is phenomenal. They're making it happen: Thirty-five controllers, shaking with laughter, rapping out orders in monotone and in beat to the Waltz of the Flowers. *India Proceed! Tango-on- the-Fly; Yankee-On-the-cross-wing-5-Dot-Squeal-and-Rye. One hundred to the Retro; muscle hurry scoot. Two hundred for the Tail Number. Echo Mike Reroute.*

It makes sense to the pilots. They must do as they are ordered.

So the airplanes dance; the music plays; and the giggling people of Britain and the world log in for a birds eye view, torn – as ever - between hilarity and pity.

Pity wins. In a synchronized blast Brian Hayse and his controllers feel it. They're overwhelmed by it. What was meant to have been a joke at Pragamar Park airport - a merry, teasing send-off of the bigwigs – has tipped into something cruel. The bigwigs are truly terrified, and Brian Hayse and his controllers can sense it, being so intuitive these days. They fall silent.

ANARCHY!

For the briefest moment, the airplanes are still.

And then something magical happens.

In a dark corner of a café in Camden Town a strange-looking fellow wearing a riding hat and rainbow coloured shorts giggles quietly to himself. He spins a little globe. And he spins it again. Faster and faster. And he thinks to himself – *what does he think?*

We don't know.

That's the joke.

In any case, the airplanes begin to levitate.

"Are they *levitating?*" cries Ozias, clapping his hands with glee.

"My God, they're levitating!" cries Sensible Su, who's watching it in her kitchen; cries Lady Stevens, who's watching it with her dog; cries Barry DeLuxe-Kelton, who is watching it in his supermarket; cry Russell Drisell and Debs Malone, and Hennrick and Grace, and the Doctors at Reading A&E, and the wagglers outside Westminster tube station, and George Houseman in his mountain schloss, and Eric Leider and David Balls in their favourite pubs, and – yes – Kitty Manage at the hairdresser, and even the Yallops, on the Downing Street lawn and... indeed, all across the world, the ecstatic cry goes up:

"My God, they're levitating!"

News spreads fast in the digital age.

The airplanes levitate. They bunch. They tilt their

noses skyward. They squeeze a little closer, and they spin, like Ferdinand's globe, like a giant tornado… up – up – up – and

A whoosh.

No crashing metal. Nothing cataclysmic. The planes fan out and fill the sky. They loop, they twirl and off they flee, in search of a place – any place - where the wind won't blow, and the answer, my friends, might never catch up with them.

And the giggling simpletons left behind…
live happily,
and wisely,
and kindly
ever after.

THE END

ACKNOWLEDGEMENTS

Thank you Panda La Terriere for the cover and the videos and the encouragement and the editorial advice and for your patience and humour and kindness and generosity and, above all, for your amazing cleverness … Thank you.

It's been quite a bumpy ride getting this book out, which makes all those who did stick their necks out – even the tiniest bit – all the more treasured. Thank you a million times – Richard Miniter, Dylan Coligan, Paola Frankopan, Florence Read, Toby Young, Zebedee de Sales, Peter and Bashie La Terriere, Eliza, Alexander, Marcia and Pierre Waugh, Tom Wells … and of course, as always, my good friend, Imogen Edwards Jones, who has never not seen the funny side.

Thank you Rick Armstrong for riding to the rescue. And thank you Rachel Topping. God Bless Fisher King Publishing.

Picture by Zebedee de Sales

DAISY WAUGH was a newspaper journalist for about 30 years. Today she teaches yoga and reads the tarot. She has written 14 novels and two nonfiction books which between them have been translated into many languages.

daisywaugh.com